Praise for the novels of

P.D. MARTIN

"Readers who enjoy hard-nosed police drama or *CSI*-style television shows will find [Sophie] an engaging character."
—*Fresh Fiction*

"A clever concoction."
—*The Age* on *Kiss of Death*

"Martin provides solid entertainment as she takes a high-concept premise and runs with it. The narrative is fast-moving, the protagonists likable, the police detail and dialogue believable and the serial killers just as evil as they need to be."
—*Publishers Weekly* on *The Murderers' Club*

"As always, Martin delivers a cleverly plotted and entertaining read, chockablock with fascinating procedural details and flashes of dark humor."
—*RT Book Reviews* on *The Killing Hands*

"A gripping read."
—*Herald Sun* on *Fan Mail*

"Well-structured and unusually imaginative."
—*The Mystery Reader* on *Fan Mail*

"Martin is a real find."
—*Women's Weekly*

P.D. MARTIN

KISS
OF DEATH

MIRA®

Recycling programs for this product may not exist in your area.

ISBN-13: 978-0-7783-2779-0

KISS OF DEATH

Copyright © 2010 by Phillipa Martin.

All rights reserved. Except for use in any review, the reproduction or utilization of this work in whole or in part in any form by any electronic, mechanical or other means, now known or hereafter invented, including xerography, photocopying and recording, or in any information storage or retrieval system, is forbidden without the written permission of the publisher, MIRA Books, 225 Duncan Mill Road, Don Mills, Ontario, Canada M3B 3K9.

This is a work of fiction. Names, characters, places and incidents are either the product of the author's imagination or are used fictitiously, and any resemblance to actual persons, living or dead, business establishments, events or locales is entirely coincidental.

MIRA and the Star Colophon are trademarks used under license and registered in Australia, New Zealand, Philippines, United States Patent and Trademark Office and in other countries.

For questions and comments about the quality of this book please contact us at Customer_eCare@Harlequin.ca.

www.MIRABooks.com

Printed in U.S.A.

One

A narrow trail snakes in front of me, lit only by the full moon. If I can make it to the road...or hide...

Low-hanging branches scrape across my face, breaking through my raised arms and drawing blood. But I can't stop. I have to keep running. Can he smell my blood?

I stumble and fall to the ground. For a moment all I can hear is the deafening thud of my heart. But then I notice it. Silence. No more footsteps hurtling down the path behind me. I pick myself up and keep running, not convinced I've really lost them.

Finally I stop, resting my hands on my thighs to try to slow my breathing. I look around at the houses perched on the hilltops to the right. They're too far away to hear or see me.

The crack of a branch on the far side of the trail frightens me. I back away. My eyes, even though fully adjusted to the night, strain to decipher my surroundings. Is someone behind that tree? I keep moving backward, but then another branch snaps behind me. I run.

Soon I hear the footsteps again. I push myself harder,

*run harder. I glance back, hoping they're farther away
than they sound. But they're not. Slamming into something, I come to an abrupt stop. I fall backward. I look
up. His face is in shadows, but I can see glistening white
teeth as he smiles.*

*Fangs dig deep into my neck, accompanied by sear-
ing pain.*

I wake up with a start, rubbing my neck. The very last
part of the dream flashes back to me…what the…? But
then I realize I've fallen asleep on the couch to a rerun of
Buffy the Vampire Slayer. Obviously its imagery spilled
into my subconscious as I was dropping off.

I drag myself over to the TV and turn it off, moving
my head from side to side to stretch my neck. Someone
in *Buffy* may have got fangs in the neck, but all I've got
is a crick in mine. Serves me right for falling asleep in
front of the box. Flicking off the lights, I make my way
into the bathroom for the usual nightly ritual—cleanse
and moisturize my face and brush my teeth. I complete
it all on remote, watching the process in the mirror like
a third-party observer.

Before going to bed I decide to do a final sweep of
my apartment. I'm always security conscious; my job and
my past make me extra careful and I often find the only
way I can sleep is to search my apartment before I turn
in for the night. I grab my gun and start at the front door,
looking through the peephole. The coast is clear outside.
From my front door I can see most of the open-plan space
of my living room and kitchen. White walls and down-
lights are made warmer by rich hardwood floors and two
French doors that lead to a large balcony—one of my
favorite features during hot summer nights. Like half of
the complex's balconies, mine overlooks the swimming
pool and well-landscaped gardens.

The open-plan space has few potential hiding spots,

so I move straight to the large hall closet. Once that's checked I head for the bathroom, even though I was in there less than a minute ago. I pull the shower curtain back with my left hand, aiming my gun low into the small bathtub. It's empty, and I move quickly to the next door—my bedroom, and the only room in the house with carpet…I love the feel of the squishy warmth under my bare feet. Dark wood furniture with a Japanese feel off-sets the cream carpet, again creating warmth in what could be a stark room. I check behind my three-panel Japanese screen, before moving to the built-in wardrobe. Opening one door at a time, I scan the clothes and also squat down to make sure only *my* shoes, facing away from me, occupy the closet. Like the rest of the place, it's all clear. As my final check I flick on the outside light and make sure no one's on the balcony.

Looking down at the Buddha that sits in the corner of the room, I say: "All clear." But I'm talking to myself, not the deity. Maybe I need a pet.

Sunday, 11:00 a.m.

On my way home from Bikram yoga—something I've discovered since moving to L.A.—my BlackBerry buzzes with an incoming call. There are only a handful of people who could be calling me on a Sunday, and when I see the number is withheld I jump to the logical conclusion—work. Still, while all special agents are always on call, as a profiler most of my work is initiated in the office Monday to Friday.

"Agent Sophie Anderson."

"Anderson, it's Rosen." George Rosen is the head of the L.A. office's Criminal Division and many of my cases come through his department.

"What's up?"

"Murder."

"Go on," I say.

"Do you know Temescal Gateway Park?"

"Uh-huh." Temescal Gateway Park is about twenty minutes from where I live and work—Westwood, L.A. I've even done a few of the park's walks.

"A body was found there an hour ago. Right on the border of Topanga State Park."

"And we've got a call already?" Police rarely call in the FBI so quickly in a homicide case, unless there's something strange about the death or the area is rural with no local expertise in murder cases—and nothing twenty minutes in any direction of L.A. is rural. There must be some other reason why the Bureau's being pulled in early. Could be jurisdiction if they suspect the killer's been active in other states or, given they're calling a profiler, it's also possible there's something unusual about the murder or the scene.

Rosen's tone softens. "You're going to love this one, Anderson."

"Really?" I lean back into the car seat and am met with the sticky sensation of sweat-drenched hair on the back of my neck. When you do yoga poses in nearly 104 degrees for an hour and a half, your body takes a while to cool down.

"It's gold." Rosen pauses again and I get the feeling he's enjoying keeping me in suspense.

I play along. "Come on. Spill it."

"Where to start… Female vic, reported missing early this morning…and there are two puncture marks on her neck."

Puncture marks? I immediately think of last night's dream, but say, "Like a snakebite?"

"Maybe. But there's another line of inquiry, too. Rumor has it a group of self-proclaimed vampires uses Temescal Park for rituals from time to time. The group's called After Dark and apparently its leader is a charismatic male, which fits the cult pattern. *If* we are dealing with a cult and it's suddenly turned violent…"

"Gotcha." I take a deep breath. Cults, or NRMs—new religious movements—if we're being politically correct, aren't my usual area of expertise, but I have studied the psychology behind NRM behavior and some of the more spectacular examples of cults gone terribly wrong in America's past. But is vampirism a religion? Maybe some people treat it like one.

Rosen continues. "Couple of months back they arrested two people who were in the park illegally, after hours. That'll be your starting point."

"Two people…that's hardly a cult."

"No, but they are part of After Dark. The two guys said they were in the park by themselves and stuck to that story, but rangers saw a much larger group dispersing." He takes a breath. "Come into the office and I'll brief you fully, then I want you to get your ass down to the crime scene."

"Yes, sir." I look down at my yoga gear. "It'll be half an hour. I'm not at home." Normally I'd head straight to work, but given my current state I need to shower and get some proper clothes on first. No way am I showing up at a crime scene in tiny shorts and a midriff top, both partially see-through from sweat.

Rosen pauses. "What the heck. It's a nice day out. Let's just meet at the scene. See you at Temescal Park in forty minutes or so."

"Yes, sir."

Interstate 5 is busy as usual, but it's moving well and I make good time back home. Within ten minutes of Rosen calling, I'm pulling into a parking spot on the street and racing up the stairs to my apartment. My shower is rushed, but while I'm shampooing and rinsing I think about the case—what little I know at this stage. A cult of vampires? This could be big. Whatever happens, it'll certainly be interesting. And how many "vampires" are there in L.A.? I've got lots of questions and no answers.

Within fifteen minutes I'm showered and dressed in gray pants and a black scoop-neck top. To this I add my shoulder holster and Smith & Wesson before popping the suit jacket over the top. Time to hit the road.

I drive north on Veteran, past the massive veteran cemetery, up to Sunset. On the corner of Veteran and Sunset a guy with a board slung over his body advertises maps to celebrity homes, reminding me that I'm passing through *that* part of town. I take a left, traveling west.

The drive along Sunset is peaceful, and as the road winds through wealthy suburbia, with large blocks and beautifully kept houses and gardens, I try to recall last night's dream. I was running through a wooded area and there were at least two people running after me, maybe three because I had people on my tail when I slammed into the "vampire." I visualize Temescal Park and try to imagine it in the dark—the area certainly fits the bill, fits my dream.

As I round a bend just near Chautauqua Boulevard, a row of tall gum trees reminds me of home. In some ways America and Australia are so different, yet you could take small sections of each country and cross-transplant them without really noticing much discrepancy. The gum trees remind me of similarities, but one trip on the I-5 would remind me of the differences. And the drive-through Starbucks here…I could have done with a few drive-through coffee shops when I was on the force in Melbourne.

I hit Pacific Palisades, and the group of shops on Sunset gives the suburb a homely, almost rural feel. I'm close, and sure enough a few cross-streets later I come to Temescal Canyon Road. I turn right into the park's entrance and am immediately met with an LAPD car.

I hold my ID against the driver-side window and

the officer waves me through. "Drive on up to the top, ma'am."

I follow his instructions and drive past a couple of parking turnoffs, until I see more cop cars and a Chevy Impala with the coroner's emblem on the door. I pull my car onto the side of the road, just after the Temescal Camp Store. A sign says Park Vehicles Only, but today it's overrun by law-enforcement cars. Rosen is holding a file in his hands and leaning on his car—obviously waiting for me.

Once I'm parked next to him, I open the door. "Is she up one of the trails?"

"Yup." Rosen moves toward me and waits while I quickly change into the runners I keep in my car.

I tie my laces. "Beautiful spot, huh?"

"Sure is."

Problem is now this park will be forever tainted with murder and with memories of last night's dream. Not all my dreams come true, but obviously last night's must have had a psychic nature.

I stand up and take a deep breath of the spring air. The temperature isn't anywhere near the daily maximum yet but it's a pleasant and fresh sixty-one degrees.

Rosen hands me the file.

I take the white manila folder. "You spoke to the homicide detective?"

"Yup. Detective Sloan from LAPD. She said to take the Temescal Ridge Trail about a mile up."

I nod and flip the file open. The first photo is a close-up of a woman's neck, with two puncture marks. "Crime-scene photos already." I raise my eyebrows.

"We are in the digital age."

I smile. "Quite."

I'd like to flick through the file's contents now, but I'm also eager to get to the crime scene. "I'll check this out later." I close the file but keep a hold of it. "Let's head up." I don't want to keep the LAPD waiting any longer—not when they've invited us onto their turf.

We make a beeline for a lone cop who seems to be on point. He stands next to a flagpole and an American flag twitches in the slight breeze above him. Around this bitumen area stand large trees—firs, oaks and sycamores—as well as smaller shrubs and a very young willow tree. Extending up behind the cop is a steep hill.

We show him our ID and he waves us through. "Take the left-hand trail, ma'am, sir."

We both thank him and follow his directions. Within three hundred feet we come to brown tourist signs indicating the different trails. We climb the couple of steps made from stone and take the left fork at the next round of trail signs, which tell us that the Temescal Ridge/Temescal Canyon trail is a 2.6 mile loop. So far the area is peaceful, but I know darkness waits for us. A woman has come to a grisly end at the hands of a murderer... or two...and it's up to us to give her justice. I know it's cliché but that's still how I see my job—bringing justice to the dead.

"Do you know Detective Sloan?" I ask Rosen as we walk up the steady incline.

"Sure. She's an old-timer. Did her stint in the Sheriff's Department but couldn't give up the chase." He lets out a little laugh. "LAPD decided to give the old gal a second running."

"Is she a fan of the Bureau?"

"I don't think she's particularly pro or anti. But she knows this case could be tricky. It's certainly unusual."

"I'll say."

Given the uphill and windy nature of the gravel trail, coupled with the dense brush, we could be a minute's walk from the scene and wouldn't necessarily see it. I tread carefully and keep to the main pathway so as not to disturb anything that may turn out to be evidence. I also keep my eye out for anything unusual. No point looking for footprints, because the area's covered in them. If the perps left their own mark on the trail last night, they would just blend in with the hundreds of others. Hopefully there'll be some more telling prints near the body.

We get to a bend in the pathway and take the turn. The path extends up for another three hundred feet in front of us to a ridge, where the trail turns again…but still no body.

I look up the hill. "Maybe it's around the next bend."

"Sloan said they're in a clearing off the trail, but that we'd be able to see them from the main path."

I nod and we keep moving upward. My heart rate increases slightly and I can feel my fatigued muscles working on the steep incline. On either side of the trail are smaller shrubs scattered amongst the trees. There are also several cacti dotted around the patches of vegetation. The path is obvious; however, it wouldn't be that hard to move off the trail and through the denser brush.

Finally, at the next corner, I hear voices. It's still hard to work out how far away they are, with the wind and mountain slope carrying the sound and distorting distance, but we're close.

Both the victim and killer, or killers, probably came up this path. There's only one way up, unless they hiked in from the neighboring Will Rogers State Park to the east or Topanga State Park from the north. But it's much more likely they parked on the street somewhere, jumped the park's nighttime barrier and made their way to the trail. The park is only open from sunrise to sunset, but I doubt the security is heavy.

"Who found the body?" I ask.

"One of the park rangers. They had a call at nine this morning from a resident who overlooks the park. He spotted what looked like torches around midnight last night and then lights again just after two. Called it in this morning."

I look around for any houses that might have a good view. From here there are only a few houses in the distance to the east, too far away to see much.

Rosen's starting to puff. "The ranger didn't think much of it, but decided to check it out anyway. It was about ten when he found the body."

Rosen called me around eleven, so things moved pretty quickly. An LAPD officer would have come down immediately to secure the scene and wait for the homicide detectives, Forensics and crime-scene photographers. The specialists would have arrived about 10:30 a.m., and the forensic pathologist from the coroner's office probably only just beat us.

Within a few minutes I can see another row of houses in the distance—one of these homes must be our witness's. I look around, taking in the surrounding area more closely. To the south is the ocean, and to the north, east and west are hills, some of which are claimed only by nature, while other slopes hold large residences or clusters of smaller houses. The views would be magnificent and I imagine it's prime real estate. Certainly nothing I would ever be able to afford on a government salary. So, the witness saw into this clearing, saw activity, but did he see anything that will help us further? All the houses are too far away for the naked eye, but if the resident has binoculars or a telescope, he may have seen much more than I glimpsed in last night's dream.

We round another bend and run into a hive of activity. Most are uniformed police officers from the LAPD, but I can also make out the forensic pathologist Belinda Frost from the coroner's office and a few plainclothes officers. Only one female in plainclothes, presumably Sloan.

In her mid to late fifties, she wears her graying hair pulled back in a neat ponytail. She's about fifteen to twenty kilograms overweight, and well-defined lines across her brow, eyes and around her lips help me peg her age. She wears a well-cut navy suit, with pants that flare slightly at the ankle. The suit's color brings out bright blue eyes and naturally rosy cheeks.

Rosen strides over to her. "Detective Sloan, nice to see you again."

"You, too, Agent Rosen."

Rosen introduces me.

"Ah, yeah. My head girl." She taps her head.

"That's me." I smile and take her outstretched hand.

She gives me two firm pumps. "Thanks for coming out so quickly."

"Thanks for calling us in."

She gives me a forced smile. While some law-enforcement officers jump at the chance to get a helping hand from the FBI, others avoid us like the plague. Sloan requested Bureau involvement but it doesn't look like she's exactly overjoyed by our presence. She's probably just covering all bases.

"So…there's our gal." She steps to one side giving us a view of the body next to Frost's crouching figure. The victim looks to be in her late teens or early twenties and is slim but curvy—a fact accentuated by her nakedness.

Frost turns around. "Hi. It's…Anderson, right?" She and I met at a conference six months ago.

"Yup. Agent Sophie Anderson." She's several feet away, so we give each other a nod rather than going in for a handshake.

"And good to see you, Agent Rosen. Out in the field, huh?"

Rosen shrugs. "Well, it was a nice day, and this case sounded intriguing."

Frost nods. "It is."

I move closer. "Any chance it's just a simple snakebite?"

"Unlikely." Frost stands up. "Snakes usually leave residual venom around the wound. I swabbed the area and my preliminary tests were clear. I'll run full tests back in the lab to be sure, but at this stage it doesn't look like we're looking at a snake."

"Was there any saliva?" Is DNA too much to ask for?

She shakes her head. "No saliva showed up under ALS, but we might get something from deeper inside the wound."

Whether the murder was premeditated or an impulsive act, the killer may have had the good sense to wipe the girl's wound clean of saliva—assuming she was, indeed, bitten as the fanglike puncture marks might suggest. Still, we might find something he missed, hiding in a crevice of the wound.

"Any sign of sexual assault?" Rosen asks.

"Rape kit was positive for semen, but at a guess I'd say we're looking at consensual sex. No bruising or tearing. And no restraint marks."

I nod, but I know it's inconclusive. Rape comes in all shapes and sizes and just because her body doesn't show signs of violent or rough sex, doesn't mean it was consensual. A gun or knife to the head—or some other threat of violence—usually ensures the victim doesn't struggle.

"Any defensive wounds?"

Frost squats back down and picks up the dead woman's arm with a gloved hand. "We've got a few scratches on her arms, hands and face, but if she ran along this trail or in this area they're probably from the tree branches rather than an attacker."

Last night's dream comes flashing back. The victim was running all right, with branches hitting her face despite her attempts to shield herself.

"I should be able to confirm that under the microscope. There'll be particles of wood or leaves."

I squat down next to her. "And cause of death?"

"Not sure at this stage."

I peer more closely at the neck wound. The two puncture marks are perfectly cylindrical and very neat, with no obvious tearing of the surrounding skin. However, the skin is red, and looks almost like a small hickey—like someone sucked on the wound. "Could it be blood loss? If we are dealing with someone from this vampire group, that's likely, yes?"

Frost screws up her face. "She looks a little pale but if she died of blood loss it's going to be a tricky one to prove."

"Really?"

"There's no way to test at autopsy how much blood is in the body and we've only got a few drops here." She points to roughly six drops of blood next to the body.

I'm surprised, but when I think about it I've never worked a case of blood loss where the surrounding area wasn't covered in blood. And the experts always specify how much blood was lost at the scene, from which they can conclude blood loss as the cause of death.

Sloan bends down next to the corpse, too. "Someone sure has made it look like a vampire, though."

"Not necessarily *look*." I scan the rest of the victim's body. "There are people who truly believe they are vampires. That they need blood to survive."

While it's possible someone wants us to *think* we've got a vampire on our hands and is recreating that scene, it's also possible that we're dealing with people who believe they are modern-day vampires. If that's the case the murder and crime scene hasn't been purposely staged, the killer has just murdered the victim in what he'd consider a "natural" way. And psychologically there's a big difference, especially in terms of a profile.

I stand up again. "Time of death?"

"Based on her liver temp and the current outside temperature, between one and four."

Frost would have inserted a metal probe through the skin and into the victim's liver to get the all-important core body temperature. While some forensic pathologists prefer to take the rectal temperature so they're not piercing the skin and organs, obviously Frost is in the liver-temperature camp.

"That time ties in with our caller." Sloan pulls herself to standing with some effort.

"What did the witness see?" I ask her.

"Lights, like torches, moving, and then later on a circle of smaller lights. I haven't been to interview him yet, but he's next on my list."

I flick the ring on my little finger. "Sure does sound ritualistic."

"Yup. Why do you think I called you in?" Her response is a little terse.

I look around at the scene. "What else have you got?"

"The ranger who found her is over there." Sloan nods at a tall bearded man in his early thirties. "He was careful with the crime scene, careful trekking in and out, and we've managed to find quite a few distinct footprints nearer to the body."

"Any idea how many sets?"

"Too early to tell. But apparently this clearing is a common stopover point for walkers. It'll be hard to tell if the prints are from last night or earlier in the week."

"Any in a circle?"

She shrugs. "We'll know more in an hour or two."

"You ID'd the girl?" Rosen bends down to take a closer look at her face.

"Yes. Sherry Taylor." Sloan leans over the body. "There was an APB put out for her earlier today. She's twenty years old, and lived in Brentwood with her parents, who reported her missing this morning."

I chew on my bottom lip. "You've done the death knock?"

She sighs and nods. "Just got back. The parents were too distraught to talk, so I'm giving them an hour or two before we start questioning them. I'm hoping they'll give us the formal ID this evening or early tomorrow. But I did take a head shot for them. It's their girl, all right."

"I'd like to sit in on any meetings you have with them, if that's okay, Detective. I need to know as much as possible about Sherry."

She nods. "I know the drill, Anderson."

"Great."

I take another look at the body, noticing her nakedness in every sense of the word—no makeup and no nail polish, which is unusual for a young woman. Did the killer or killers remove these things? It might tie in with the sacrifice angle—she had to be pure.

Sloan moves us away from the body.

"Ever seen anything like this before?" I ask her.

"No. I've seen a lot of bizarre things in my time, but nothing that implicates vampires. You?"

"My vampire viewing's limited to *Buffy*."

She gives a brief chuckle before letting out a heavy sigh. "The vampire mythology has always held a sense of intrigue, but it's everywhere now."

I nod. "And vampires are part of our consciousness from an early age. Even *Sesame Street* has The Count."

"Humph…I never thought of that." She looks back at the body. "Young women like Sherry…they think vampires are cool."

I stare at the body, too. "I bet Sherry Taylor didn't think it was cool when she was running for her life."

Two

Our caller lives on El Medio Avenue, overlooking both Topanga State Park and Temescal Gateway Park. Sloan and I pay him a visit together, leaving the crime-scene techs and Sloan's partner, Detective Carey, to finish processing the scene. Rosen also leaves, opting to go back to the office and finish some paperwork, and Frost will be heading off with the body soon, too. Every forensic pathologist is different, but an hour or so at the scene is plenty for most.

Sloan and I take my car, and I turn off Sunset onto El Medio Avenue. The incline starts immediately, and within less than half a mile we're on the crest of a large hill. From the road, the houses seem like larger suburban blocks, and their impressive views are hidden behind their bulk. It'd be nice to have a state park in your backyard. Especially so close to downtown L.A.

"What do you think one of these would go for?"

Sloan lets out a whistle. "Dunno...not exactly in my budget." She peers out the window for a second look. "You'd have to be talking five to ten million, maybe more."

"Ouch."

"Uh-huh." She pauses, looking at the street numbers. "We're almost there. Third house on the right."

I pull into the curb outside number 922.

Sloan unbuckles her seat belt. "We're looking for Mr. Heeler."

The house is a gray weatherboard, with white easels and window frames. It's set back from the road a little more than some of the other houses, with a large concrete driveway leading to a double garage under the main residence. We walk along the driveway, up the two porch steps and knock on the white door.

A man in his late fifties answers. "Yes?" With one word, one breath, the stench of stale alcohol hits me. Great.

"This is Agent Anderson, and I'm Detective Sloan from the LAPD." We both show our IDs.

"Of course." He gives them a cursory glance with bloodshot eyes. "I'm Andrew Heeler. Please come in."

Heeler is wearing khaki pants, a black shirt and bare feet. His graying hair is short, accentuating his round face and dark brown eyes. He takes us past a staircase and a living room on the right, into a large kitchen and open-plan space that looks out onto a deck…and the park.

"Wow," I say. "What a view."

He stops and looks out the windows. "Yes. It's magnificent." He sighs. "Except when kids are fooling around down there."

"The people you saw were young?" Sloan asks.

"I don't know. I'm just assuming." He turns around to us. "Tea, coffee?"

Sloan and I both accept the offer of a coffee.

"Take a seat if you like." Heeler motions toward a large black leather couch.

Once we're both sitting, Sloan asks Heeler how long he's lived here.

"Over fifteen years now."

We start off with idle chitchat, ready to move to the more serious questions as soon as is polite and strategic. There's no reason why Mr. Heeler would be on edge, but it doesn't do any harm to make sure he feels at ease despite the official presence.

Sloan leans back into the couch. "You married, Mr. Heeler? Kids?"

"Widowed." He flicks the brewer on and comes over to sit opposite us. "And I've got one son who's twenty-five."

I eye the telescope on the deck. "You're a star-gazer?"

"Sometimes, yes. Although it only tends to be a couple of times a month these days. Just laziness, I guess."

I smile. "Is that what you were doing last night?"

A few beats of silence go by before he responds. "Yeah." He seems uncertain, like he's trying to piece the events together. "I think it was around midnight…I went out to use the telescope, but then the lights in the park caught my attention."

"Can you take us through exactly what you saw, Mr. Heeler?" Sloan asks.

"Um." He stares out the window. "I went out to have a look at the stars—" he points toward the balcony "—and was adjusting my telescope's position when I saw something out the corner of my eye." He waves his left hand off to the side. "There were about six or seven lights." Another pause. "Looked like torches. They were moving. I went to take a closer look, but it was too dark, despite the full moon. All I could see were lights and shapes… figures."

"Your telescope looks pretty powerful, Mr. Heeler," I say. "You couldn't see any more detail?" The telescope is very thick, and my understanding is that the larger the diameter the more magnification.

"Oh, I wasn't looking with my telescope. It's far too powerful for that. I got out my binoculars." He moves back into the kitchen. "I can't believe…" He pauses mid-sentence, a cupboard door open and one coffee mug in his hand. "I can't believe a girl was murdered." He shakes his head and gets another two coffee cups out. "I thought it was kids, fooling around. I never thought…"

"Of course, Mr. Heeler. We understand."

We wait in silence for a few minutes while he organizes the coffee and then heads back over to us.

Sloan takes the cup he hands her. "So could you see if the figures were male or female?"

He hands me my coffee. "No. Too dark, too far away." He starts to sit down but then bounces back up. "Sorry, cream and sugar?"

"Cream for me," I reply.

"Both for me."

He places his cup on the coffee table and grabs a bowl of sugar and some milk from the kitchen, putting them both out on the table. "Where was I?"

Sloan empties a heaped teaspoon into her coffee and stirs. "You couldn't see if the figures were male or female. It was too dark, too far away."

"Ah, yes." He takes a sip of coffee. "I figured there was no point calling the police just for some kids playing around in the park. I gave up on the stars because of the cloud cover, but finished my drink on the deck before coming back inside to watch TV."

"What were you drinking last night, Mr. Heeler?"

Sloan's question seems to take him by surprise. Eventually he tells us it was vodka.

Sloan leaves it for the time being. "You told the park ranger that you saw a circle of lights?"

"Yeah, that's right. I fell asleep on the couch and woke up around quarter after two. When I was locking the balcony door I saw the lights. I actually think it was candles rather than torches the second time."

Candles? A circle of candles is an instant, striking visual.

He stares at his coffee, mesmerized. "Although I was half asleep at that point."

We have to ask ourselves the question a defense lawyer would ask Heeler if we put him on the stand—half asleep or in a drunken stupor?

He takes another sip of coffee. "This morning I started thinking about the lights and decided maybe I should call the park and let them know." He shakes his head. "But I didn't think it was serious. I thought maybe there'd be beer bottles or other trash that the rangers might want to clean up."

Sloan gives him a nod. "Mind if we have a look from your deck?"

"Sure."

The view is even more spectacular when we make our way out, with an expanse of trees and greenery stretching for miles. Just looking at the valley makes me take a deep breath—clean air in L.A. At least, it feels clean.

"That's where I saw the lights." Heeler points down, right about where I'd expect our crime scene to be from this angle. Maybe he wasn't that drunk after all.

"Have you got those binoculars, Mr. Heeler?" Sloan asks. "I'd like to see what you saw."

"Sure," he says and heads inside.

Sloan leans on the deck railing, facing me. "What do you make of him?"

I wince. "Not exactly the most reliable witness."

"Did he fall asleep on the couch or pass out?"

"He has got the spot about right, though." I point to the area.

"True." Sloan pauses. "If it was a circle of lights, what do you think that means? For the investigation?"

I raise my eyebrows. "I'm sure we've come to the same conclusions…some sort of a ritual or sacrifice. Could be that Sherry was in the center of that circle, dying or dead when Mr. Heeler saw the lights—candles or not."

Sloan is silent but gives a small nod. I know she's at least entertaining this possibility, otherwise she wouldn't have requested a Bureau profiler.

A minute or so later, Heeler returns with the binoculars. He holds them out, not sure who to pass them to.

Sloan tips her head to one side. "You go."

I take the binoculars and scan the terrain, looking for the crime scene. Within less than ten seconds I've found it, but I can see what Heeler means. While I can see there are people moving around and I'd be able to count them and even determine their gender, if it was dark that would be impossible. Even assuming they were holding torches or candles. "It's a good view, a good vantage point, but in the dark…" I hand the binoculars to Sloan.

She focuses them on the scene. "I see what you mean. It was a full moon last night, but lots of cloud cover."

Back inside, Sloan asks Heeler if he's ever seen anything suspicious before.

He shakes his head. "Not like that. I know the park is closed from dusk to dawn, but people do get in. Occasionally I might hear something—people yelling, that sort of thing. I imagine it's frequently underage drinkers…maybe teenagers looking to have sex?" He turns the last part into a question.

"Yes, that's right, Mr. Heeler," Sloan answers. "The park rangers often find empty bottles, but mostly around the entrance, not this deep into the park. And they have also interrupted a few…passionate moments." She drains the rest of her coffee. "I think that's it." She looks to me for confirmation.

I nod and we head for the door.

At the door, Sloan turns back to Heeler. "There is one more thing."

"Yes?"

"How much do you think you drank last night, Mr. Heeler?"

He looks at his feet and kicks the ground. "I did see something."

"You admitted to being half asleep and under the influence. How can you be sure you saw a circle and candles last night?" Sloan's pushing him, like a lawyer would.

Leaning one hand on the door frame he stares at the ground. "I guess...I guess I can't be one hundred percent sure, can I?" It didn't take much for Heeler to cave.

We both thank him for his time.

Back in the car, I start the engine. "Doesn't look too good."

Sloan shakes her head. "He'd be hopeless in court, and that's if *we* buy his story."

"He was obviously a little drunk last night, but he did pick the right spot."

"Mmm..." Sloan's not convinced. "His call did lead to the body, but I think a healthy amount of skepticism is warranted about the other details."

Sloan may not believe Heeler, but I do. After all, I have the added benefit of last night's dream. I have to assume I was Sherry, running away from multiple perps and I definitely saw lights and vampire fangs.

"Let's say he's right." I pull the wheel hard and U-turn, heading back down El Medio Avenue toward Sunset Boulevard. I'd programmed the Taylors' address into my navigation system before we left the park, so now I follow the directions to their Brentwood house. "He thought there were about seven or eight torches, so that could be the number of perps we're dealing with. And that could tie in with this group, After Dark."

"Do you think After Dark could be a cult?"

"Maybe. It'll be interesting to see the dynamics. Is it a cult or just a group of like-minded individuals? Did the cops who worked the trespass case interview any of the other members besides the two they caught? Or get some other names, even?"

"They got the leader's, one Anton Ward. Someone should have sent that stuff across to Rosen. You didn't get it?"

"Sorry, yeah. I haven't had a chance to look through it yet. It's on the backseat."

"The two offenders were Larry Davidson and Walter Riley of WestHo. They were fined for trespassing, but that was the end of it. The investigating officers flagged the possible wider vampire angle but felt that both Davidson and Riley were harmless, and there's nothing illegal about 'being' a vampire. The two admitted to being part of a group called After Dark, run by Anton Ward, but stuck to their original story—that they were in the park alone."

"Even though the ranger saw other people running off?"

Sloan nods. "Yup."

"So they were protecting the group. Either of their own volition or under orders."

"Yeah." Sloan's thoughtful. "A single leader makes it more likely it's a cult, yes?"

"Not necessarily. While one of the characteristics of new religious movements is an enigmatic leader who has complete control over his followers, most everyday groups have some sort of leadership hierarchy. A school has a principal, a board of directors has a chairman and even a group of hobbyists will have one main person who directs the action."

Sloan turns to me. "We're hardly talking schools, corporations or hobbies here, Anderson."

"I know. The cult angle is a definite possibility."

Silence for a beat before Sloan says, "Even if After
Dark is a cult, it doesn't mean they're involved in anything illegal, let alone murder."

I stop at traffic lights on Sunset. "Point taken. And
I have to admit I don't know much about the vampire
subculture, although I know it's associated with the Goth
culture."

"Me, neither. Nightlife in L.A. is always interesting." She smiles. "According to the files, Davidson and
Riley had been to a Goth nightclub before they were
arrested."

I raise my eyebrows. "Maybe we should check it out…
check out their nightclub scene." I stifle a smile, imagin-
ing Sloan and I dressed like we are now and flashing our
badges at a Goth club.

Sloan smoothes down the fabric on her pants. "I know
we've got the so-called fang marks, but I'm more interested in her love life as a starting point."

Sloan's going for the most common angle—the boyfriend or husband did it. She's also not putting much faith
in Heeler as an eyewitness, but she could be right about
him.

"I agree we need to check out any boyfriends or exes,
but I'd still like to know more about this scene. We could
talk to the managers or bar staff at these clubs. See what
they know about After Dark." I pause, my mind jump-
ing ahead to the evening. "Maybe even drop by tonight,
when they're setting up…"

Sloan's nose crinkles. "Maybe. But like I said, I'm
more interested in the men in Sherry's life, not to mention
building a timeline of her movements last night. What
happened between 9:00 p.m., when she left her family
home, and her entrance into Temescal Gateway Park?"

Sloan's thinking of the case like most cops would—
trace the victim's last known *movements*. And while we
do need to do that, my interest as a profiler focuses more

on human *behavior*, including group dynamics and the lifestyle of a subculture our victim may have been involved in.

"What if Sherry Taylor was a Goth? Could be she was at one of the clubs herself last night."

Sloan shakes her head. "Not if the family photos I saw this morning are anything to go by."

"She could have been hiding it from her parents, or maybe it was recent." I'm starting to feel like I'm flogging a dead horse, but my dream points toward multiple perps, not a boyfriend.

We sit in silence for a bit before I say, "The parents reported her missing this morning, right? Shortly before the ranger found her body?"

"Uh-huh. It was logged at eight this morning. An officer took the report over the phone, and issued an APB for Sherry and her car. But it would have been a few days before the report made its way to the Missing Persons Unit."

I nod. The procedure for a missing persons case varies depending on the situation. If Sherry had been five years old or if there had been evidence of a struggle in her home, resources would have been thrown at the case immediately. But as a twenty-year-old woman, chances were that she simply stayed over at a friend's or boyfriend's house and didn't tell her parents. Her name would have been in the system; but only if the parents were insistent enough would someone have checked the hospitals and police system this morning to make sure Sherry hadn't been hospitalized or arrested. And then if Sherry still hadn't turned up, the case would have been assigned to someone in the LAPD's Missing Persons Unit within a couple of days. Their next move would have been to interview the parents and close friends, start making inquiries at her workplace and maybe on Wednesday or Thursday they would have started with credit card traces and phone records. Now, with Sherry dead, Sloan will start the ball rolling on all of those things, though, sadly, toward a different end than finding *her*.

The navigation system prompts me to take a right, and within a few minutes we're pulling up at the Brentwood home of Mr. and Mrs. Taylor. As we drive up to the gated entrance, the house is visible in the distance. It's a large two-story home, bagged white with a distinctive Mediterranean feel, wood-stained window- and door-frames and an outside timber shutter on each window.

Sloan presses the buzzer at the gate and after only a few seconds a male voice answers.

"It's Detective Sloan from LAPD again, sir."

"Right…come on in." The voice is distracted; I assume it's Mr. Taylor's.

A brick-paved driveway snakes toward the house, past beautifully landscaped gardens. We follow the driveway and park near the front door, opposite a small fountain. The water feature is blue-tiled, with white mosaic-style images of mermaids on the internal walls. Small umbrella palms line a path from the driveway to the front door.

We're not even up the two steps when a man in his mid to late forties opens the door. He wears thick but trendy framed glasses, a red T-shirt and black jeans. His face is plagued with despair and I know instantly that I'm looking at Sherry's father.

Sloan clears her throat. "Thanks for seeing me again, Mr. Taylor."

He nods.

"This is Special Agent Anderson from the FBI."

He tries to force a polite smile, but it comes out more like a grimace as he shakes our hands. "Come in."

He leads the way through a foyer section of the house. I've changed back into my regular work shoes, and they make a loud clipping sound on the slate, the noise triggering a vision.

Sherry opens the front door, takes off a pair of high heels and tiptoes along the hallway.

The vision is probably an accurate insight of Sherry coming home late one night, or perhaps it was a regular Friday and Saturday night routine for her. Regardless, I doubt it's of consequence to the case. It certainly doesn't give me a sense of what might have happened to her last night.

The house is very light and mostly open—a staircase to the right, almost immediately at the entrance, and to the left the space is barely separated into rooms. From here I can see a living room, dining room and expansive kitchen. Mr. Taylor takes us through the first room, which seems like a formal living room or sitting room, through the dining room and into the kitchen. To the right of the kitchen is another living space, which opens up onto a large deck with double doors and a swimming pool. He takes a seat on one of the leather couches and we sit on the couch opposite him.

Sloan props on the edge of the couch. "Is your wife here, Mr. Taylor?"

"Um…yes. She's upstairs…lying down."

"It would be better if we could talk to you together."

He rubs his hands up and down his thighs. "I don't know if Mandy's up to it, Detective."

"Please…it *is* important. Would you mind asking her if she could come down? Even for a little while." Sloan's voice is both sympathetic and authoritative. She realizes it's much more likely for a mother to know about a young woman's comings and goings than a father.

Taylor nods in an absent manner and he heads up the stairs.

"Still in shock." Sloan leans back on the couch.

"Yes." I look around at a few family portraits.

"Looks like there are two girls. Wonder where the other one is."

"College age, so chances are…"

I nod. "I don't know if we're going to get anything useful out of them in this state."

Sloan shrugs. "I'd like to get this moving sooner rather than later." She looks at her watch. "And we've still got a few visits to get through today."

Footsteps are audible coming down the stairs and we're both silent.

Mr. and Mrs. Taylor enter arm in arm, although it's obvious she's leaning heavily on him. She's dressed in expensive-looking casual wear that could double as gym gear. A common look in L.A. Black leggings show off her slender but muscular frame, accompanied by a halter-neck top and sweater. Her mass of red curls is pulled into a ponytail and a few stray curls hang at her face. A glance at her eyes tells me she's had something to take the edge off the pain or to help her get closer to oblivion—perhaps Valium or she could have knocked back a few drinks.

"I'm sorry," Mr. Taylor says, "it's Detective Sloan and…"

Sloan introduces me again, this time adding in my role in the investigation as a behavioral analyst.

"Behavioral analyst? A profiler, right?" Mr. Taylor leads his wife over to the couch opposite us.

"Yes, sir."

They take a seat.

Mrs. Taylor turns blurry eyes our way. "So you'll help catch the…the monster who did this to our baby girl?"

Sloan jumps in. "We've asked Agent Anderson to consult on the case. She will draft what's called an offender profile and help us interrogate suspects. We'll also use her expertise for our media strategy."

"Media strategy?" Mr. Taylor seems confused.

The services a profiler offers law enforcement cover

four areas—media strategy, offender profile, interrogation strategy and prosecution strategy. We may be asked to consult on all or just one of these areas.

"The way the media portrays the case may affect the killer's behavior, and thus how we track him or her down," I explain. "I'll liaise with the media to help contain their reports as much as possible. Try to control how Sherry and her murder are reported to the public."

Mrs. Taylor lets out a large sigh. "Can we just get this over with?" Her speech is slurred.

"I'm sorry. My wife's just taken a sleeping pill."

"That's okay, Mr. Taylor. We understand."

He nods, seemingly relieved that we're not judging his wife for popping a tablet at lunchtime.

I smile at them both and try to gauge how much time we'll get with Mrs. Taylor veering toward the incoherent. We should get at least a few minutes out of her, maybe ten.

"Can you tell us a bit about Sherry?"

He looks at a photo of her on the mantelpiece. "What do you want to know?"

"Did Sherry work?" I ask. According to Sloan there was no employer noted on the missing persons report but I'd like to confirm it with the Taylors. We need to talk to as many people who knew Sherry as possible, and place of employment is usually a good start.

"No. She was at UCLA. Drama."

"An actress." Sloan doesn't seem surprised. Then again, in L.A. lots of people are hoping to become actresses, especially pretty young women like Sherry Taylor.

"That's correct, yes. She has some talent, too." Mr. Taylor has none of the usual parental bragging in his voice. He seems detached, more like he's making a professional observation.

"You're in the industry?" I ask.

"Yes. I'm the lead writer and producer on *Stars Like Us*."

Impressive…I don't watch much TV, but I know the half-hour sitcom is doing very well in the ratings and I see billboards for it everywhere.

"So Sherry grew up with it. I presume she's already appeared on TV?" Sloan still hasn't taken out her notebook. I doubt she's relying on my notes so she must have a superb memory.

"No." Mrs. Taylor's voice floats. "Brian won't let either of the girls act until they've finished college." It's hard to tell from Mrs. Taylor's tone if she has any strong feelings about her husband's rule. Perhaps there's a slight exasperation in her voice.

"I've seen what acting does to children…adolescents. Especially girls. And that's not what I wanted for Sherry or Misha."

College isn't exactly the most wholesome environment, either, but I keep my mouth shut. Mr. Taylor doesn't strike me as particularly strict, certainly not authoritarian, so I'm guessing this was one of his few rules—something he wouldn't, or couldn't, bend on.

"She was only a couple of months away…from finishing college and being able to fulfill her dream." Silent tears fall down Mrs. Taylor's cheeks. Before the sleeping tablet they probably would have been hysterical tears but now they're masked by medication and numbness. She's been beaten—by life, by God, by whatever you believe in. Although I try not to, I can't help but think of my mother. Even though I was nine years old, I don't remember the day they told us that my brother John's body had been found. It was a year after his disappearance and I already knew he was dead anyway…I saw it in a nightmare. But I have managed to block the death knock from my memory.

"What about Misha? How old is she?"

Sloan's question brings me back to the present.

"She's eighteen." Mr. Taylor rests his hand on his wife's knee. "There's only nineteen months between the girls." He stands up and takes the photo he looked at earlier from the mantelpiece. "This was taken at Christmas." He hands it to Sloan.

The family sits around a table, with a turkey in the center. I also notice a bottle of Louis Roederer Cristal in an ice bucket, and that Sherry has on full makeup and nail polish.

"Just the four of you?" I ask.

"Yes." Mr. Taylor nods. "I'm an only child and my parents are both dead, and Mandy's parents spend Thanksgiving with us and Christmas with Mandy's brother in New York."

I take another look at the photo. "Sherry lived here with you, correct?"

"Yes. She would have loved to live on campus, but I didn't see the point...not when UCLA is a five-minute drive."

"And Misha?" Sloan passes the photo back to Mr. Taylor.

"Misha's studying music...in New York." He stares at the photo.

"I see."

"Have you told her yet?" Sloan asks softly.

The question brings another onslaught of tears from Mrs. Taylor, and this time not even the medication can control them. "I can't...I can't do it."

"We can't wait any longer, Mandy." Mr. Taylor turns to us. "I was just about to call Misha when you arrived."

"Without me?" Mrs. Taylor stands up and pulls at her hair with one hand. "How could you?"

"We have to tell her." Taylor's voice is soft.

Mrs. Taylor hesitates for a moment before sinking back into the couch and holding her head in her hands. "Maybe you're right. She has to know, and Lord knows I can't bring myself to say those words."

We're all silent for a few beats.

"It's not going to be on the news or anything, is it?" Mr. Taylor gently places the photo back on the mantelpiece. "Misha can't find out like that."

Sloan shakes her head. "Not Sherry's name, no. We won't release those details until you've made a formal identification at the coroner's office." She pauses. "Perhaps tomorrow?"

"No, I need to see her as soon as possible." He's still looking at the Christmas photo. "Need to see my baby to believe it's really her."

We nod, and Sloan says, "I understand."

Silence again.

"Sherry…" I pause. "Was she outgoing? Shy?"

"More outgoing, I guess. She certainly had a lot of friends."

"She was an extrovert." Mrs. Taylor looks up. "She drew people to her and was loved by everyone. Sherry and her friends often spent time over here—I always opened our house to them."

"Did she have a best friend? Someone she was particularly close to?"

"Desiree Jones. They've known each other since high school. Both charming, social girls."

"We'd like her details. And the contact details of anyone else close to Sherry."

Mrs. Taylor manages to stand up. "Of course. I'll get my address book." She strides out of the room, but I can tell the deliberate movement and poise take her full concentration.

When she returns, she reads out a few names and we take down the details.

"Anyone else? Perhaps that you don't have contact details for?"

"I know all Sherry's friends. Sherry and I are very close."

I haven't decided yet if Mandy Taylor is a more open, progressive mum, or if she's one of those mums who live their lives through their children. Could be she had to be part of Sherry's social life, almost think of Sherry's friends as her friends.

"What about a boyfriend? Was she seeing anyone?" Sloan asks.

"No." Mrs. Taylor fiddles with her address book, which now sits closed on her lap. "She dated Todd Fischer for three years, but they split up just before Christmas."

Sloan leans on the couch's arm. "She still in contact with him?"

"No. It was a clean break."

"You know who broke it off?"

"She did. Told me it just didn't feel right anymore."

"Anyone new on the scene?" Sloan asks.

"No."

"But she wouldn't bring a new guy home to meet the folks. Not if she'd only been with him a few weeks," Sloan says.

Mrs. Taylor's eyes move slowly from Sloan to me. "Maybe not. But she would have told her mom." She takes a few quick breaths, holding back tears. "I told the police officer when I reported her missing this morning that something was wrong, seriously wrong. My baby girl wouldn't just not come home one night. But he didn't take me seriously." The tears come again.

"There was an APB put out for Sherry and her car. He certainly *did* take you seriously, Mrs. Taylor." Sloan's voice is soft.

Mr. Taylor looks at his wife, then back at Sloan. "Why weren't you out there, looking for her?"

"We were, Mr. Taylor." Sloan edges forward on the

couch. "The APB meant that every LAPD officer on the street was on the lookout for Sherry and her car."

While that's true, in reality there would have been several APBs out during any one shift, and one for a missing twenty-year-old girl wouldn't have taken priority. The LAPD would have been too busy with shootings, rapes, active arrest warrants, drugs and their normal urgent duties. In fact, the Taylors were lucky to get an APB at all. A twenty-year-old on a Friday or Saturday night with no evidence of foul play…no police department in the world was going to be genuinely concerned. And 99.9 times out of 100 they'd be right.

"It was the APB that allowed us to identify the victim as Sherry so quickly," Sloan continues.

After a few minutes of silence I try to move us on. "Did Sherry have any new friends that you met or that she spoke about?"

Mrs. Taylor looks up and shakes her head. "No."

"Any changes in her behavior?"

"Not that I noticed." Mr. Taylor looks to his wife for confirmation. Maybe he's an absent daddy—too busy at the office to get to know his kids. Not that unusual.

"She was her normal happy self. Looking forward to finishing college, spending the summer in Europe and then coming back to break into the acting business. She had it all ahead of her." A few more sobs escape from Mrs. Taylor. "She was really happy." The last sentence is particularly slurred, perhaps from the sedatives kicking in or perhaps from grief. Either way, our time with Mrs. Taylor is coming to an end.

"Just a few more questions now," Sloan reassures.

"Was Sherry part of the Goth subculture?" I ask. "Interested in that scene at all?"

"No." Mr. Taylor manages an amused snort. "She was into designer labels…and I've got the credit card bills to prove it."

"What about her friends? Anyone she knows a Goth?"

"No." Mrs. Taylor's brow furrows. "What's this got to do with Sherry or…what happened?"

"It's just a line of inquiry we're pursuing." Sloan clasps her hands together.

Mr. Taylor sits next to his wife again. "Do you suspect someone? Someone from this group?" He says it with distaste.

"We're not sure at this stage. As soon as we have more, I'll let you know, I promise." Sloan's voice is casual, almost dismissive.

"What about makeup? Did Sherry usually wear much of it?"

Mrs. Taylor shrugs. "Just the normal amount for her age. Base and a bit of lipstick during the day, and if she was going out at night she'd wear eye makeup, too."

I nod. "And what about her nails?" Judging from the photos I've seen at the house, I can easily envisage Sherry as a regular for manicures and pedicures.

Mrs. Taylor confirms my suspicions, telling me her daughter nearly always wore polish on both hands and feet.

"Do you happen to recall if she was wearing any last night?"

"Um…" Mrs. Taylor stares at her lap. "I'm not sure…I can't remember."

"That's okay." I put my hand out to her, even though I'm not within reach. "There is one other thing, Mr. and Mrs. Taylor."

They both look at me.

"I'd like to see Sherry's room. It'll help me get a better understanding of your daughter."

Mr. Taylor stands up. "Of course." He looks at his wife. "You wait here, honey."

Good call—I'm not sure Mrs. Taylor could cope with being in the girl's room at the moment.

We follow Mr. Taylor back toward the front door and then up the stairs. The second story of the house is decorated in a similar fashion to downstairs, although carpets and a few paintings give it a homier feel. Taylor leads us into a bedroom toward the back of the house.

"This is Sherry's room." He looks into the room but then looks away. "If you don't mind, I'd like to wait with my wife."

Sloan gives him a small smile. "Sure. And don't worry...we'll be very careful in here."

"Thank you."

Once Taylor's gone, Sloan and I start snooping. Sherry's bedroom is covered in posters, with one wall dedicated to photos of Sherry and her friends and family. The room looks busy and lived-in, but still tidy.

Sloan studies the posters and photos. "Nothing Goth-looking."

"No." I move over to Sherry's desk. "We should get some computer techs onto this." I glance at Sherry's laptop, which is plugged in but switched off.

"I'll log a request this afternoon."

A glance at the bookshelf reveals that Sherry is into mostly fantasy and sci-fi, but there are also a couple of paranormal titles on the shelves. A closer look reveals two books set in the vampire world.

"Check this out." I hand Sloan a copy of Kerri Arthur's *Full Moon Rising*. "Maybe Sherry *was* secretly part of the Goth world."

Sloan reads the back of the book. "Doesn't mean a thing, Anderson. Vampire fiction is in. And *Sesame Street*, remember? You said it yourself."

Sloan's right, but it's still interesting that we found something from the vampire world in Sherry's room. I make a move for her wardrobe. If Sherry was involved in the scene, she'd have to keep her clothes somewhere. I flick through the hangers, but find nothing except top-line designer clothes of the commercial variety. "Nothing in here."

Sloan pulls out the second-last drawer of Sherry's chest of drawers. "I haven't found anything yet, either."

I look around the room, soaking it in, while Sloan finishes going through the drawers.

"Nope." She closes the bottom drawer. "Nothing unusual, and no Goth, either."

I sigh. "And nothing else that gives us an idea of how Sherry might have wound up at Temescal Gateway Park last night."

"No." Sloan leans on the chest of drawers for a moment, also looking around. After a few seconds she says, "Guess we're done here, at least for the moment."

"Yeah. Do you mind if I soak up the atmosphere for another couple of minutes? I'll join you in a sec."

"You gonna get into her head?" Sloan gives me a slightly teasing smile.

"Something like that."

"Good luck." She moves toward the door. "I'll let the Taylors know not to touch Sherry's laptop and that someone will come by in the next day or two to pick it up."

I nod. "Thanks."

Profilers always try to walk in the victim's and killer's shoes, but obviously for me I want time alone to try to induce a vision. I had my first experience of seeing something that was about to happen when I was eight, but then this ability of mine went underground...until I was working the D.C. Slasher case nearly two years ago. Since then it's been a bumpy road, fueled first by my own denial and then my acceptance. I can nearly always induce *something,* but the usefulness of what I see is often questionable. Like Sherry sneaking home one night—every young woman's done that. Still, I always use my gift on a case and sometimes it does help.

Sitting on Sherry's bed and staring at the collage of photos on her wall, I'm conscious that I don't want to be long, but I try to push that sense of hurriedness away. Instead I take long and deep breaths, close my eyes and concentrate on relaxing.

I'm tired and my vision is blurred. People gather around me, but I can't make out any faces…everything is so hazy. There's a voice, a deep voice, but I can no longer focus on the words.

The vision is brief, but the sense of wooziness makes me wonder if Sherry was drugged. The routine tox screen will answer that question. However, there was nothing in the vision that indicates time. While it may be related to her murder or the unaccounted hours prior, it could also be something entirely different. Maybe she took some recreational drugs at a party weeks, months or years ago and for some reason I tuned into that. Plus, there's nothing that can definitively tell me this vision was necessarily about Sherry. Logic suggests that it was—I am in *her* room, after all—but I've learned over the past couple of years not to take anything for granted when it comes to my visions.

I head back downstairs, not entirely sure how long they may have been waiting for me. Usually the length of my vision is in line with how long I'm "out" for, but sometimes it can take me several minutes to experience a ten-second flash.

As I'm coming down the stairs I hear Mr. Taylor saying, "I'd like to go now."

When he comes into view, I can tell by his slight rocking motion that he's agitated; he shifts his weight from side to side. Sloan's card is in his hand.

"Of course, Mr. Taylor. Whatever you'd like."

He takes a deep breath. "But I need to ring Mish first."

"The coroner's office is on Mission Street and me or my partner will meet you there, but it may be best if you don't drive."

"I haven't...I haven't taken anything, Detective."

"I know, sir." Sloan puts a hand on his shoulder. "But you're not yourself...no one can be under these circumstances. Most people get someone to drive them." Again, Sloan pulls together just the right tone of voice—sympathetic yet somehow commanding. "How's 3:00 p.m.? That'll give you time to call Misha."

He nods and takes a deep breath. "Thank you."

On the way back to the car, Sloan says to me, "Mom's real confident she knows her girl's social life."

"Yes. But it'll be interesting to speak to Sherry's friends, especially the best friend."

Sloan nods. "And you think the makeup and nail polish thing is significant?"

"Maybe. It could tie in with the human sacrifice theory—perhaps our perps felt the need to cleanse her as part of the ritual."

"And if it's not a sacrificial death?"

I shrug. "If the killer removed the polish and makeup, could be he wanted his victim to look more natural for some reason, or it could even be a sign of remorse."

"Remorse?"

"It's possible he felt guilty and needed to care for the body in some way."

Sloan's brow crinkles. "Guess I can see that." She pauses. "You said if the killer did it...who else could have removed the polish and makeup?"

"Sherry. She may have been a willing participant... up to a point."

Sloan nods and punches a number into her mobile phone. "How's it going there? Uh-huh...yup. We've just finished with the Taylors. Can you meet Mr. Taylor at the coroner's office to identify the body at 3:00 p.m.? Great. Thanks."

"Any news from the crime scene?" I unlock the car while Sloan walks around to the passenger side.

"Not really. Body was only released an hour ago." She opens the door and we both climb in together before she continues. "Photographs are complete but the Forensics guys are still looking over the area. And they're still casting and cataloging the footprints."

"I wonder if we'll have a better idea of how many people were involved in Sherry's death once they're done." I start the car, unsure where we're going next.

"I'm not hopeful. The ranger said that most walkers take the detour for the view, which means a lot of non-relevant data."

"But did our perps know that?" I pause. "They certainly didn't try to hide the body."

"True."

We're both silent, focused on the evidence.

"So where to?" I ask.

"The ex-boyfriend."

"We should also speak to the best friend, and I'd like to check out a Goth club and the two guys who were done for trespassing, Riley and Davidson."

Sloan lets out a sigh. "Busy day. I've also got a load of paperwork I need to start on. Credit card and bank account information for Sherry, plus I'll put a request in for phone records."

"I hear you." Sloan's not the only one with paperwork. I still haven't read the file and I'm keen to get more info on Anton Ward and the L.A. vampire scene.

"Maybe we should split up. You can do the FBI-profiler thing, and I can look after the LAPD's interests." There's a hint of frustration in her voice, but that ties in with the occasional vibe I'm getting off Sloan—like maybe she's regretting calling the FBI to her turf.

The problem is I want to be there when she questions the ex-boyfriend and the best friend. They'll give me a good insight into Sherry, and victimology is always my starting point.

"Let's see how we go. The best friend is around the corner, so we could visit her first, then the ex, and after that I'll get caught up on the file and you can log your paperwork," I suggest.

"Sounds like a plan." Sloan fastens her seat belt.

I pull into the traffic and head for Desiree's address. I don't mind if we don't get time for Riley and Davidson today, because I'd like to soak up the atmosphere at one of the Goth clubs—that would be a better introduction to the scene than interviewing two members in their homes.

"I'm actually considering going to one of the clubs tonight...dressed up." I need to look like one of them, otherwise I'll be too conspicuous.

"Really?" Sloan gives me a sideways glance. "You're thorough."

"If After Dark is involved, I need to get an insight into the culture."

She shrugs. "I'll definitely pass on that one. Besides, I'm guessing the Goth scene doesn't have too many men or women in their fifties."

I laugh. "How old are Riley and Davidson?"

"Riley's twenty-two and Davidson's twenty."

I wince. "Maybe *I'm* too old."

"Ward's in his thirties." Sloan takes out her mobile phone. "I'm just going to check in with the officer who took the missing persons call this morning." She dials a number and after a few minutes on hold she's redirected to his mobile—he's off duty. She places her phone on the center console between us.

"Is this Detective Saporo?" Sloan asks.

"Yup."

"It's Detective Sloan calling from Homicide. I believe you took a missing persons report on Sherry Taylor this morning."

"That's right." A heartbeat of silence while recognition hits…he's getting a call from a homicide detective. "Oh, shit. You're *friggin' joking.*"

"Sherry Taylor's body was found in Temescal Gateway Park this morning."

"Dammit." Saporo draws the word out forcefully. "I thought…I mean she's twenty and lived with her parents. Shit! She told me her daughter wouldn't just stay out all night."

"No one would have handled the call any differently given the circumstances. In fact, you read the situation well to even issue the APB." Sloan moves on quickly. "Where's the missing persons report at now?"

"I presume it's in the Missing Persons Unit's queue." He swallows loudly.

"Okay, thanks. I'll let them know. You followed procedure, it's just this was the one in a thousand."

Three

Like Sherry Taylor, Desiree Jones lives with affluent parents in Brentwood. The house is significantly smaller, but in a much more ornate, almost Tuscan-villa style with wrought-iron window fittings and bright ceramic patterned tiles running beneath each window. While set back from the road and with a tall fence, the property doesn't have a security gate.

An older Mexican woman answers the door.

"Hola." Sloan smiles.

"Hola."

In my eight months in California, I've noticed the influence of the Latino culture on the city. With over twenty-eight percent of the population Latino, guess I'd better learn a few words in Spanish.

Sloan flashes her badge. "We're here to see Desiree Jones."

"Sí. Come in." She looks concerned, but also curious, and I wonder if Desiree and her family have been contacted by the Taylors. When we left them fifteen minutes ago they hadn't told their other daughter about Sherry's

death, so I doubt Desiree knows. Still, she likely knows Sherry's parents were concerned about her.

The woman beckons us inside and takes us through to the first door on the left. Unlike the Taylors', this house has more traditional rooms—one door in and out.

"Coffee? A cold drink?"

Sloan and I both accept the offer of a coffee and a couple of minutes later Desiree and her mother appear at the doorway. Mrs. Jones is a tall, striking African-American woman and while Desiree has inherited her mother's beauty, she's more than a head shorter.

Sloan does the introductions and Mrs. Jones and Desiree both look uncertain rather than devastated. This is definitely a death knock. I've made my fair share of them working homicide in Melbourne, but it doesn't get any easier. How do you prepare someone for this type of news?

"Have you found Sherry?" Mrs. Jones asks.

"You haven't spoken to the Taylors today, ma'am?" Sloan confirms.

"No. Is…is everything okay?"

"I'm afraid we've got some bad news…"

"Yes?" Mrs. Jones wraps her arms around her daughter.

Sloan takes a breath. "Sherry Taylor was found murdered this morning in Temescal Gateway Park."

Desiree immediately bursts into tears and turns to bury her face into her mother's chest.

Mrs. Jones pulls her daughter closer and strokes her hair. "No, that's not possible." She bites her lip. "Are you sure it was Sherry?"

"Mr. Taylor is making the formal identification at three, but I'm afraid we're quite certain it's her. I'm sorry."

The maid enters, with a tray in hand. She immediately

parks the tray on the coffee table and speaks in rapid Spanish to Mrs. Jones.

"It's Sherry, Gabriella. She's…dead. Murdered."

Gabriella responds in Spanish and makes the sign of the cross before moving to Desiree and stroking her cheek gently. She's obviously close to the family, close to Desiree.

Desiree manages to speak. "How…how was she killed?" She turns around.

"We're still waiting for an official cause of death from the coroner."

While the statement is true, Sloan is purposefully leaving out the details of blood loss and puncture marks.

"Was she…" Desiree takes an audible gulp. "Was she raped?"

"Again, we're not able to say conclusively at this stage."

We sit out the silence until Desiree and her mum both manage to sit down.

"Please, your coffees." Mrs. Jones motions to the tray. A good host, even in distressing times.

"I'm sorry we have to give you this news." I sit down. "I'm sorry for your loss."

They both nod and after several seconds of silence Mrs. Jones motions to the coffee again.

I take a cup and add a generous amount of milk. "How long have you known Sherry, Desiree?"

"We met in middle school." She bites her middle fingernail. "At Edna Hill Middle School. And we've been best friends ever since."

"How often did you see her?" Sloan scoots back on the couch and takes a sip of the coffee she's just poured.

"Pretty much every day."

"The girls were inseparable. They were either over here with me or at the Taylors' with Mandy most days. Plus the girls are at college together, too."

"UCLA?"

"Yes." Desiree nods her head, but she's barely present in the conversation. "We're both studying theater... acting."

Mrs. Jones bites her lip. "I can't believe...can't believe she's gone. She was such an amazing young woman. Vivacious, kind, charismatic." She gives Desiree a squeeze.

"When did you last see Sherry?" I ask Desiree.

"Friday afternoon."

"You didn't see her last night?"

"Desiree was here." Mrs. Jones shakes her head. "My husband just got back from a one-week business trip and I wanted the family to be together. Maybe if I hadn't insisted..."

Desiree puts her hand on her mother's knee. "Mom, Sherry didn't ask me to go out with her or anything."

Mrs. Jones nods and strokes her daughter's cheek.

"So, what did you do Friday?" I ask.

Desiree rests her elbow on the couch arm, moving closer to her mother, who's sitting on the arm with her hand resting on Desiree's shoulder. "We met at UCLA and rehearsed for a performance we've got coming up. After that we went for a bite to eat at Noah's and then came back here and hung out for a bit."

I nod. There's a Noah's Bagels in Westwood Village, close to both UCLA and the FBI building. On the odd occasion that I go there for a bagel, the place is packed with students. "What time did she leave here?"

"About eight."

"And what about last night?" Sloan takes a sip of her coffee. "Sherry went out...do you know where? Or who with?"

"She had a date."

"What?" There's a hint of annoyance in Sloan's voice. "Did you tell Mr. and Mrs. Taylor this?"

Desiree hangs her head. "No. Sherry swore me to

secrecy. Told me it was someone new and it was just a date."

"Honey, why didn't you tell me? Why didn't you tell Mandy and Brian when they called this morning?" Mrs. Jones stands up and starts pacing.

I keep my voice even so Desiree doesn't have all three of us coming down on her. "Do you know who the date was with?"

"No. It was some guy she met recently."

"Where did she meet him?"

Desiree lets out a tearful sigh. "I'm sorry, I don't know. She wouldn't tell me." She looks up at her mum. "I'm sorry, Mom."

"But she didn't come home, Desiree. What were you thinking?"

Desiree bursts into tears. "I thought she must have stayed over at this guy's house, and I couldn't tell her parents that...." She takes a gasping breath between sobs. "And...now...Sherry's...dead."

Mrs. Jones lets out an exasperated sigh but then kneels down next to her daughter, holding her hand. "It's all right, honey. You weren't to know."

"And the Taylors called you at seven-thirty this morning?" Sloan asks.

The phone call must have been part of the missing persons report, because it's not something we discussed with the Taylors.

"Yes. But it was so early. If she'd stayed the night with this guy..."

It's fair enough. A Saturday-night date could easily run into the early hours of the morning.

"So you weren't worried when her parents told you they couldn't get her on her cell?" Sloan crosses her legs.

"No." Desiree sweeps a chunk of hair off her face and

tucks it behind her ear. "I figured she forgot to charge her cell or turned it off for, you know, privacy."

There's something Desiree's not telling us and I don't know if she's hiding it from her mum or from us. I contemplate the direct approach. I could just ask Mrs. Jones to leave the room, tell her I want to talk to her daughter alone. But it may backfire and make Desiree clam up.

"Do you know if this guy went to UCLA?" Sloan asks.

"I don't think so."

I lean forward. "Did you ever see him?"

Again she shakes her head. "I'm sorry."

The two girls seemed to tell each other everything, so it's unlikely that Sherry would hide a date from Desiree without good reason. A married man, perhaps? Or someone from the Goth world that Sherry was hiding from her friends and family.

I take out my card. "If you can think of anything else, Desiree, about Sherry or her mystery date, please call us. It's very important."

Sloan and I offer our condolences again and thank Mrs. Jones for her hospitality before heading back to the street and my car.

"She's hiding something," I say to Sloan once we're inside.

"Agreed. But what? And is it something that could get Sherry killed?"

Sunday, 3:30 p.m.

Todd Fischer lives with his mum in E 219th Street, Merit-Carson. Their small house is nestled between two much larger and newer properties. And while the houses on either side show off new paint jobs, new roofs and are both double-story, the Fischer residence is single-story with a pebble-mix finish that was once perhaps a high

contrast of white, black and gray stones, but is now decid-
edly gray all over. The red tiled roof is in need of repair;
however, the small front garden is neat and well kept. The
house is very different from the Taylor residence.

I look at the house. "I wonder how Todd and Sherry
met. Doesn't seem to me like they'd move in the same
circles."

"No." Sloan gets out of the car and pulls down her suit
jacket, which has ridden up. "Do you think he knows?"

"Not unless the Taylors have started the ring-around.
Or got someone else to start it."

Sloan moves to my side of the car. "Let's have a chat
before we tell him then, huh?"

I nod, but feel a little torn. If Todd is our man, it makes
sense to hold back and see if he hangs himself. An innocent man wouldn't know Sherry was dead, and wouldn't
hide anything. At the same time, if he *is* in the clear, it's
pretty cruel to question him for God knows how long
without telling him his ex-girlfriend's dead. Still, it goes
with the territory. Our duty is to Sherry Taylor.

We cross the road and knock on the door. After a
minute or so a woman in her forties, dressed like she's
twenty, answers.

"Yeah?" She chews gum loudly.

We take out our ID and identify ourselves.

She narrows her eyes. "What do you want?" There's
a hint of both annoyance and concern in her voice.

"We'd like to talk to Todd Fischer. Is he home?"
Carson is a long drive if Fischer's not in, but unannounced
visits are always more effective in this game.

"Todd!" the woman yells without moving farther into
the house.

After a few seconds with no response she yells again.
"Todd! Get your ass down here."

Heavy footsteps sound above us, moving toward the

stairs. "Mom, I told you not to disturb me." Todd's feet appear on the steps. "What is it?"

"Cops are here to see you."

"Oh… Okay." He doesn't seem surprised.

Once he's halfway down the stairs he comes into full view. Todd Fischer is about six-one, tall and lanky, with black hair and pale skin that looks paler against his red lips and rosy cheeks.

"Is this about Sherry?" He moves off the stairs and toward us.

His mother turns to him. "Told you no good would come out of dating some rich bitch."

He gives his mother a scathing look. "Give it a rest, Mom."

"Whatever." She pops the gum in her mouth.

He turns back to us, hands shoved deep in his pockets. "She's really missing then?"

We don't have a chance to answer before his mum blurts, "You don't have to talk to them, Todd."

"I'll handle this, Mom. You go back to…whatever you were doing."

She gives us a sneer. "Whatever." She chews her gum noisily and moves off to the left and the background hum of a TV set.

"We can talk in the kitchen." Todd leads us in the opposite direction, through an extremely messy room that is presumably the dining area but is sparsely furnished and covered in old newspapers and bric-a-brac.

Following him through a swinging door, we move into a seventies-style kitchen. The decor is red and white, which makes it look almost retro rather than dated. A splash of paint and new appliances and it could look good. Certainly a few less dishes in the sink would help.

Todd looks around and sighs. "Sorry about the mess." He shakes his head. "Can I get you a drink? Coffee?"

At the rate we're going, I'll be getting the caffeine shakes soon.

"Sure," I say politely.

Todd flicks on the kettle and then starts opening cupboards, obviously searching for clean cups. "I can't believe Sherry's really missing."

"Have you spoken to the Taylors recently?" Sloan takes a seat at the kitchen table. The chairs are metal-framed with patterned vinyl for your butt and a curved, thin backrest. They remind me of our kitchen set during my childhood. But ours was brand-new, and the Fischers' is over thirty years old.

"They rang this morning. To see if Sherry was with me." He takes three cups from the pile of dirty dishes, squirts dishwashing liquid into each of them and runs the hot-water tap for a minute before half filling each cup.

"When did you see her last?" Sloan asks.

He takes a dish brush to the cups. "Last night."

Last night? Could Todd have been the mystery date? It seems unlikely Sherry would lie to her best friend if she was going out with her ex.

"The Taylors didn't know that, did they?"

He shakes his head. "Sherry doesn't want them to know."

"Why?" Sloan leans her elbow on the table.

"She doesn't want her mom getting her hopes up."

"So you get on well with the Taylors?"

"Real well. Mrs. Taylor is, was, like a mom to me. It's been hard not seeing them for the past few months." He takes a chair, puts it beside the counter and stands on it. Reaching into the very top cupboard he withdraws a packet of Oreos and a small plate.

"Your hiding spot?" I give him a smile.

"Uh-huh. Mom would eat them in one sitting if she knew they were here."

"Really?" Todd's mum is less than ten pounds overweight.

"Don't let her fool you. She binges for a few days, then hardly eats for days on end." He shakes his head. "It's crazy."

Sloan moves around, unable to get comfy in the chair. "Was last night the first time you've seen Sherry since you broke up?"

He gives a little snort. "Hardly. Sherry and I split up four months ago, but we've still been seeing each other."

"Sexually?" Sloan's tone is harsh.

Todd winces. "I love Sherry, Detective. And I always will."

"Was the feeling mutual?" Sloan's voice is softer now.

He sighs. "Not exactly." He rinses the cups and pulls a plunger down from a high cupboard before leaning on the sink. His shoulders rise and fall in a labored breath. "She was obsessed with that professor of hers."

"Professor?" Sloan's voice is casual, but I know her curiosity is truly piqued—as is mine.

"Yes. She had a crush on him. It's why she broke it off with me." He places three scoops of coffee into the plunger and fills it with boiling water. "She said if we were meant to be together she wouldn't have feelings for any other guy."

"Do you know his name?"

Todd turns around. "Carrington. He's her acting professor." He stares at his shoes. "I guess she could be with him."

No, she's not with Carrington…she's in the morgue.

So far I'm only getting a good vibe off Todd and I'm finding it hard not to tell him that Sherry's dead.

Sloan, on the other hand, doesn't seem bothered. "Tell us about last night. What time did you see her?"

"Late. About midnight."

"Did you have a fight?" I ask.

"No." He slowly pushes the plunger down. "But she was…different." He looks up again. "She called me around midnight and she was upset."

"Go on."

"We arranged to meet in Santa Monica." He pours out three cups of coffee and places them on the kitchen table before opening the fridge and peering inside. "Dammit." Closing the fridge he looks around, his eyes finally resting on a carton of milk on the counter. He shakes his head. "How many times do I have to tell her to put the milk away?" He picks it up from the counter and smells it before looking up at us. "I'm sorry, but it is fine." He puts the milk on the table.

I get the distinct impression that this mother-son relationship doesn't have a mother in it. I often wonder how women like Todd's mum get their babies past the first two years of life. Then again, sometimes they don't.

"Whereabouts did you meet in Santa Monica?" I ask, curious as to how close they were to Temescal Gateway Park.

"There's a little spot we used to go, right where the oceanfront walk starts."

I look at Sloan, hoping she'll know the area.

She nods for both my benefit and Todd's. "I know it. Not too far from Temescal Gateway Park."

That places Todd and our victim right near the crime scene. Could I be wrong about him?

Todd doesn't pick up on the reference. If he's seen today's news he'd know a woman's body was found in the park this morning, but so far the reports haven't carried her name.

"Go on." I give him a generic prompt rather than asking a question that would lead us down a specific path.

"She wouldn't tell me what was wrong. I comforted

her, held her and told her I loved her. And then about ten minutes later she was all hot and heavy." He looks down and stares into his coffee cup. "I knew she wasn't herself and I did try to stop things a few times to make sure she was okay. But she was insistent. Voracious even. I'd never seen her like that."

"Do you know where she'd been earlier in the night?"

"At some Goth club. Researching an acting piece for class."

"Really?" I keep my voice casual, even though the link between the victim and the Goth culture is big news. It could place her right in After Dark with vampires.

He smiles. "She was all decked out in the gear. I didn't even recognize her at first…but she was in her car, so I knew it must have been Sherry. I wondered if that was why she was so…you know. The outfit sure was sexy."

"What else did she say?" I ask.

He shrugs. "Not much. We were busy."

"Did she behave differently during sex? Besides being more assertive?"

"Not really—um, what do you mean?" His face reddens slightly.

I take us down the Goth and vampire path. "You know, anything kinky? Like a desire to drink blood?"

"No!" His coffee cup connects heavily with the table and he scrunches his face up. "It was just research. She wasn't into that scene."

"So," Sloan says, "you had sex, then what?"

"She said she was tired and wanted to go home. I tried to find out what had upset her, but she said she was fine."

"And do you think she was?" Todd and Sherry were together for a long time. Hopefully he knew his girlfriend well enough to know if she was hiding her true feelings.

"I'm not sure, to be honest. She seemed okay, but Sherry's an exceptional actress."

"So what time did she head off?"

"About one."

We've filled in part of Sherry's timeline for last night at least from midnight to 1:00 a.m.—assuming Todd is telling us the truth. And we've probably found the source of the semen from the postmortem rape kit.

"Did you use a condom, Todd?" I ask.

"No." He looks down. "Stupid, I know. But neither of us had one and Sherry assured me the timing was safe… you know, in terms of her cycle." He looks up again. "Hang on, what's with the question about condoms?"

I take a deep breath. I give Sloan a quick glance and once I have a little nod from her I start. "I'm afraid we've got some bad news, Todd."

His brow furrows. "What do you mean?"

I lean toward him. "We found Sherry, but she's dead. Murdered."

"What?" He stands up, sending his chair flying backward. "No, you've got it wrong! She can't be dead."

I stand up, too, and rest my hand on his shoulder. "I'm sorry, but it is Sherry."

He's silent for a bit. "Do her parents know?"

"Yes. We informed them a couple of hours ago."

He blows out a breath and runs his hand through his hair. "I can't…I can't believe it. I was with her like twelve hours ago." He paces.

Sloan and I are both silent and the silence gives Todd enough time to get up to speed. He stops pacing abruptly.

"Oh my God…you think—" he swallows hard "—you think *I* had something to do with this? That's why you didn't tell me straight away."

Sloan looks up. "So far you were the last person to see her."

"But I didn't kill her! I *loved* Sherry."

Unfortunately in our line of work, love is often the reason people kill, not the reason they don't. As a behavioral analyst my cases tend to be more complex—serial killers, serial rapists, cold cases—but Sloan would be lapping up the circumstantial and physical evidence. After all, if Sherry's got Todd's DNA in her and he admits to seeing her at 1:00 a.m., right near Temescal Gateway Park...

Sloan stands up. "We'd like to take a DNA sample for comparison. It's just a swab inside your cheek."

"Just because I had sex with her doesn't mean I killed her."

"Of course not, Mr. Fischer. And your cooperation with the DNA certainly indicates you've got nothing to hide."

He nods slowly. "Okay."

Sloan turns to me. "I've got a kit in the car. I'll be back in a sec." She walks out, quickly, perhaps worried Todd will change his mind.

"You'll do the DNA now?"

"Yes, Todd. Like Detective Sloan said, it's just a little swab from the inside of your cheek. It's quick and painless."

He nods. After a minute or so he says, "What time was Sherry killed?"

"We're not sure yet."

Sloan enters, paper and evidence bag in one hand and a small plastic vial in the other. She puts the paper on the table in front of Todd. "Have a read through that, Mr. Fischer, and then sign at the bottom."

Sloan and I both take a seat. I purposely avert my gaze from Todd, and Sloan follows suit. Keep it nice and relaxed in case he suddenly gets jumpy. But our fears are unfounded—he quickly reads the form and signs it.

Sloan unscrews the vial. "Open wide please, Mr. Fischer."

Todd does as instructed and Sloan uses the cotton-bud end to scrape the inside of his cheek, before slipping it back inside the container, sealing it and placing it in the evidence bag.

"That's it." She gives him a quick smile.

He looks at Sloan, then me. "Now what?"

"We'll take this to the lab for comparison with the evidence we found on Sherry's body and we'll be in touch."

"I still can't believe she's…dead." He takes a deep breath and his body tenses with grief. "You will find whoever did this, won't you?"

"We hope so, yes." Sloan knows better than to make guarantees or to tell him that he's still one of our prime suspects. Agreeing to give his DNA and admitting he saw Sherry last night don't make him innocent.

"So, as far as you knew, she was heading home at 1:00 a.m.?" I confirm.

"Yes. That's what she said, and she drove off in that direction."

"And she never mentioned what she was upset about?"

"No."

We thank Todd Fischer for his time, give him our cards and leave, picking our way over the piles of old papers and magazines that cover the floor between kitchen and front door.

"Sorry about the mess," Todd says at the door. "I've given up trying to keep it even half-decent looking."

"That's fine, Todd." I hold my hand out. "Thanks for your help."

He shakes my hand and Sloan's before closing the door.

In the car, Sloan buckles up. "So we've got an ex-boyfriend who admits to having sex with her only a couple of miles from the crime scene. It's not looking good for Todd Fischer."

"I don't know." I start the car. "My gut instinct says he's innocent."

"Maybe. But it sounds like there was a new man on the scene and maybe Fischer was jealous…and angry."

"What about the bite marks? They clearly point to someone from the vampire community. And now we've got confirmation that Sherry had some contact with that world. Even if it was just for research."

Sloan raises her finger. "But Todd knew. He seems like a smart kid to me. Smart enough to make it look like a vampire attack."

Four

Once I've dropped Sloan, it's on to the Federal Building and my desk. In the end we decided the professor had to wait. Sloan needs to start logging her requests and getting the DNA sample moving and I want to find out more about Anton Ward and vampires. Besides, I'd like to interview Carrington at UCLA. It'll be interesting to see how he responds to a police and FBI visit in the middle of a class.

At my desk I open the file and turn over the first few crime-scene photographs. Rosen printed them out on regular paper, but the digital images are high resolution. The next document in the file is on Sherry Taylor, starting with the missing persons report. According to the report, she'd told her parents she was going out with Desiree Jones last night—but Desiree was with her family and had no idea she was Sherry's cover. I bet that shocked Mrs. Taylor. And despite this, she still seemed so confident that she knew her daughter's associates and comings and goings. You'd think her faith would be starting to crumble a little bit. So where was Sherry from 9:00 p.m. to midnight last night? At the Goth nightclub like Todd

Fischer said? Or was there some other mystery date? These are questions we need to answer, but first things first…the file.

I read through the three-page missing persons report filled out by Officer Saporo from the LAPD. Even though she'd really only been missing for a few hours when the parents reported it, Saporo still did it by the book. He wasn't too worried about a twenty-year-old still being out at eight on a Sunday morning, but there's no legal require-ment to wait twenty-four hours or any other specified time in California. Saporo classified Sherry's disappear-ance as Missing/Lost rather than as a runaway, parental abduction, stranger abduction or disaster victim. While it's possible she was abducted by a stranger, there was no evidence to suggest that. According to the form, Sherry Taylor was last seen by her parents leaving the house at nine last night. She was wearing tight Guess jeans with an eveningwear-style, short-sleeved top—black with lots of beading—and a leather jacket. The clothing doesn't help us much, given Sherry was found naked, although it does tell us she wasn't dressed for a Goth nightclub…at least not when she left her parents' house. So she either changed after she left, or Todd lied.

The next section of the form relates to any companions the missing person was with, but in the case of Sherry she left the house alone and we don't know who she may have seen after that—except for Todd. Information covering Sherry's car has been completed in the next spot, includ-ing the fact that her Toyota Celica hasn't been found. I give Sloan a call to confirm.

"Sloan, it's Anderson. Don't suppose Sherry's car was at our crime scene?"

"No. It doesn't look like she drove herself to Temes-cal Gateway Park. Unless someone else drove the car away."

"And her cell phone wasn't found?"

"No," Sloan confirms. "According to the parents, they were ringing her cell every ten minutes or so, from about seven this morning. It was going straight to voice mail."

"Does it have a GPS unit?"

"No." She pauses. "I do have some news."

"Uh-huh."

"Our footprint experts have finished on-scene and identified three different sets of footprints that could be part of a circle around the body. Two are only partials, but one is more complete."

"Go on."

"They'll run them against shoe databases, but we've got a women's size eight and what looks like a men's eleven and a men's eleven or twelve."

"It's a start." Although the shoe sizes are all very common. Hopefully something more specific will come from the imprints themselves.

"Problem is these prints were found amongst a lot of others. Given how much that clearing was used, any defense attorney's going to smash them in court."

I grimace. If Sloan's repeating the forensic expert's words "could be part of a circle," she's right—that's not good enough for court.

"Okay, thanks."

I hang up and move back to the form and the details of the complainant—in this case Mr. and Mrs. Taylor—and then on to the more detailed information about Sherry. Again, nothing particularly stands out. The last two sections are for forensics data, but they're blank, as you'd expect when the report had just been logged. Soon enough they would have added credit card checks and phone records and then, if suitably concerned that foul play was

a factor, they would have assigned a computer technician to start the laborious process of looking for clues on
Sherry's laptop. But for a twenty-year-old, that may have
been weeks away.

Next in the file Sloan pulled together for Rosen and
the Bureau is all the information on the trespass charge
and the preliminary information they dug up on Anton
Ward, once they made the link between the two tres-
passers, After Dark and Ward. The file contains a print-
out of Ward's driver's license, as well as an article *LA
Weekly* did on him and After Dark a few months back.
It's a feature article with a large photo of Ward and on
the other side of the page is the After Dark logo. It's a
pentagram enclosed in a circle with the word *After* written above it and *Dark* below it.

According to the article, Anton Ward was born Brett
Simons in Virginia. He was educated at Stanford, but inherited his parents' substantial fortune when they were
both killed in a car accident when he was eighteen. Ward
is thirty-two, single, with no children. A large photo for
the article shows me he's extremely good-looking, with
raven-black hair that drapes across his dark blue eyes
and pale skin. Could be hair dye, contacts and makeup.

Or maybe the *LA Weekly* Photoshopped the file. Who knows?

I ring up Mercedes Diaz from the Bureau's Cyber Crime Division. Mercedes is my workout partner and a good friend.

"Hey, Mercedes."

"Hi, Soph. What's up?"

"Sorry to bug you on a Sunday, but do you mind running a background check for me?"

"Sure thing. Hold on a sec while I fire up my laptop."

"You mean it's *not* on?"

She laughs. "Hey, I'm not that bad."

In my experience, most computer techs are addicted—in and out of work. Unlike the chef who never cooks at home, computer analysts seem to spend countless hours on their computers.

"Okay. What do you want?"

"Give me everything you've got on Anton Ward. According to an *LA Weekly* article he was born Brett Simons in Virginia but you better check that, too."

"Police, travel, education, investments, newspapers?"

"All of it."

"Okay." She's already typing speedily on her keyboard. "I'll e-mail you everything I find. Give me about thirty minutes, an hour tops."

"Man, you guys are fast."

"It's not us…it's the computers."

In reality it's both. The computers may store the information, but techs can get in, and out, quickly.

"What you working on anyway?" she asks.

"Murder case. Temescal Gateway Park."

"Sounds like you're having a good weekend."

I smile. "You could say that."

"Keep an eye on your BlackBerry."

"Will do."

I hang up and decide to start by researching the different clubs before moving on to Ward and After Dark. I soon find a Web site that lists Goth clubs around the world and do a quick check for L.A. On Thursday nights it's Perversion in Hollywood, Fridays is Ruin, Saturdays is Bar Sinister and Sundays is Malediction Society. If Todd Fischer is telling us the truth Sherry must have come directly from Bar Sinister. I ring the club and leave a message, asking for a return call as soon as possible.

Both Malediction Society and Ruin are run out of the same place on Wilshire—the Monte Cristo. Looks like I'll be heading down there tonight—if I decide to go through with it. The clubs don't seem to have dedicated Web sites, but they're all on MySpace and Facebook. Malediction Society's page features an advertisement-style layout, with posters of upcoming events and DJs that play at the club. The other clubs use a similar approach.

Next I move on to Ward and After Dark. My Google search comes up with a few articles on the group and the man himself, but nothing much that's not already in the fledgling file. Next, I log into my minimalist profile page on Facebook and do a search for Anton Ward. Sure enough, I find a few Anton Wards and soon pinpoint the group leader. The profile image on Facebook has him dressed in tailored pants and a skintight plum sweater, leaning on a grand piano. The image is more conservative than I'd imagined—like he's trying to show off his wealth and hide any more Gothic tendencies. It's also a very small picture—I can't access his full details unless I send him a friend request that he accepts. And, for the moment, I want to fly under the radar. If I decide it's worthwhile, I may set up a fake Facebook profile to see if I can get additional info. Next I search on his group's name, After Dark. I discover that Ward's set up a Facebook page, which I can view without having to join. I read the main blurb:

After Dark is a group of enlightened individuals who have embraced their real calling in this world—vampirism. Based in L.A., the group is headed by the self-made Anton Ward, who saw the need to band together with his fellow vampires and give them somewhere safe to meet. After Dark meets once a week and provides a mentoring program for all its members. The organization also helps people cross over into their new lives as vampires and matches vampires with willing donors. At the moment, our exclusive group is physically based and we purposely keep numbers low. However we will shortly be launching an online group so that After Dark can have a national and global presence. For more information, e-mail anton@afterdark.com.

I have a quick look through thumbnail pictures of the page's fans and the other basic information that Ward has posted on the page. He hasn't included a lot of details about the group or its members; rather, he's covered the basics and requested that people e-mail him with their interest in the forthcoming virtual group. It's not exactly an empire, but it could feed his ego, if not his wallet.

Next I search MySpace. With no need to "friend" him first, I find Ward's profile page quite quickly and this time have instant access to his vital statistics—at least those he self-reported. Then there's also a longer "about me" section, a link to his blog and some more pictures. I flick through these images and find some that better fit my mental image of the man, including one in which he's wearing contacts that make his eyes glow eerily.

He's got two hundred and twenty friends on MySpace, including quite a few of the Goth-inspired clubs. Overall, the theme for women is definitely corsets, dark hair, pale faces and red lips.

I could spend hours clicking the friend links and reading about Ward's online network, but I've got too much to get through before hooking up with Sloan again. Plus I've got enough initial info on him for now. While I'll reserve final judgment until I meet Ward and his group members, at this stage I see two possibilities for Anton Ward. One, he's a conman, someone who saw an opportunity to surround himself with devoted members who pander to his ego. Or two, he believes whatever teachings he may pass on to his members, believes he's a vampire. Guess I'll find out which soon.

Either way, until I discover more about Anton Ward and his group, it'll be difficult to classify them. On the surface they seem to fit some definitions of a new religious movements—they're a small, non-mainstream group that revolves around a single leader. NRMs are often associated with extremist behavior and their lifestyle is usually seen as unconventional in some way, and Ward and his group tick that box. Vampirism is extremist behavior, even in today's society where it's got a chic factor. But are they a cult? Does Anton Ward have complete control over his followers? The group didn't come onto the law-enforcement radar until Riley and Davidson were arrested—no hint of illicit or illegal activities, no missing person reports filed by family members, and so on. And even if they are an NRM, it doesn't mean they're violent or capable of murder. Many NRMs function with no incident. It's just that the ones that go spectacularly and tragically wrong get lots of media attention.

The question is, then, if After Dark is a cult, is it a destructive one?

A destructive cult tends to have one charismatic leader, uses deception in recruiting, uses thought-reform methods to effectively brainwash its members, is isolated from the rest of society, distinguishes between their kind and the rest of the world and strictly controls members' daily routines. But from what I know so far, this group isn't isolated, geographically at least. Riley and Davidson live in WestHo and Ward lives in Los Feliz. And having not met Riley or Davidson, it's difficult for me to decide if they're the "type" to be attracted to a new religious movement. From a psychological perspective, cults can give people a sense of belonging and a sense of purpose—two things people are striving for these days. Likewise, an NRM can guide people in their behavior—tell them what's right and wrong—and some individuals would rather feel guided, controlled even, than alone. But if After Dark is a destructive cult, its members could be convinced that killing a woman in a ritualistic way is okay, even required. Members don't usually question their leader's instructions. Charles Manson and his "family" are a classic example. In 1969 Manson convinced four of his members to kill Sharon Tate and four of her friends. These cult members followed their leader's directions without question, despite the fact that Tate was five months pregnant. They believed Manson represented the Second Coming and was infallible; and he convinced them that the act of killing another human being was simply releasing them from their physical bodies. Murder was not a heinous crime in their minds.

Jonestown is another famous example of the hold a charismatic leader can have on his disciples—and its disastrous results. Reverend Jim Jones founded the People's Temple of California and even managed to rub shoulders with some of America's most powerful individuals. Before long, nine hundred and seventeen of the cult's members were killed in what initially looked like a suicide pact, but investigators soon realized that about two hundred died voluntarily and the rest were murdered by fellow members under the direction of Jones. Even those that killed themselves did so at Jones' direction. Such is the power of charisma.

I check my e-mail and notice that Mercedes has sent me the full file on Ward, but before I look at that I decide to research new religious movements a little more, concentrating this time on the typical personality types of members.

An hour later, I check in with Sloan.

"How's it going?" I ask.

"Getting there. I've put through all the paperwork for Sherry's credit card records and phone records, plus I've logged a request for a computer forensic technician to get onto Sherry's laptop."

"Great. And the DNA?"

"Personally dropped it in."

I fill in Sloan on my recent activities, including the online information I found out about the clubs.

"It's a whole other world, huh?"

"You bet. Tonight's Malediction Society and I thought I might pop in around seven to talk to the staff." I'm hoping to find a manager or someone there, but if I decide to go tonight as a Goth, I'd also like to get the lay of the land before I turn up in a part of town I don't know very well.

"You do know it's Sunday night, Anderson?"

"I know. But the next Goth night isn't until Thursday."

She's silent for a bit. "I guess it can't hurt. If Todd is telling us the truth, it makes sense to check out the Goth angle, too."

"Uh-huh. I've also got some info on Ward. I haven't reviewed it yet myself, but I'll e-mail it through to you."

"Thanks."

"If Sherry Taylor did go to a Goth club last night, it must have been Bar Sinister. Hopefully there's surveillance footage somewhere to prove it. I've left a message on the club's answering machine."

"Good. Let's see if Todd Fischer's story checks out."

Sloan's keeping herself open, a little, to the possibility that vampires were involved in the murder, but at the same time she's running down one of her prime suspect's stories.

We arrange to meet at Malediction Society before hanging up. Time to find out more about Anton Ward. As I'd expect, Mercedes has been thorough. She was able to confirm many of the details in the article, including the fact that Ward was born on September 7, 1977 and his real name is Brett Simons. He changed his name to Anton Ward when he was twenty.

Her search on birth records brought up a copy of his birth certificate, which lists his parents as Laura and Jack Simons. They had no other children, and died when Ward was eighteen. She's also e-mailed me copies of their death certificates, a few newspaper articles on the car accident that killed them, as well as the police report for the crash. The report notes that it looked like Jack Simons fell asleep and veered off the road. His wife died instantly and he was announced dead on arrival at the local hospital. Neither speed nor alcohol was involved in the accident.

Jack Simons was a wealthy entrepreneur, who ran businesses in real estate, both residential and commercial. He was responsible for several large developments on the East Coast, covering Massachusetts, New York, Rhode Island and Virginia. He was also a large player in the stock market and on his death his estate was valued at over $300 million. While ten percent went to charity, the rest went to his sole heir, Brett Simons, aka Anton Ward.

I'm just about to move onto Mercedes' findings from the property records when my BlackBerry buzzes. I hit Answer without looking at the display.

"Agent Anderson."

"Hi, honey. It's me."

"Hi, Darren." I know it's cliché, but just hearing his

voice makes me feel warm and fuzzy. Detective Darren Carter and I met on a case that took me to Arizona a year and a half ago and we've been doing the long-distance dating thing for just over three months now.

"I'm at the airport. Cab, given you're not here?"

Uh-oh…I totally forgot. "Yeah, if you can grab a cab that'd be great." I chew on my bottom lip.

There's silence for a beat before he says, "You forgot I was coming, didn't you?" There's a hint of annoyance in his voice.

"No… Kinda." I take a breath. "I'm on a case. Murder victim, found this morning."

"You're working on a Sunday? Thought it was just us homicide cops who worked hard."

"Ha, ha—*you're* off duty…not exactly working hard."

"Yup. Three days off to spend with my lovely girlfriend."

I wince, wondering how much time I'll actually get to spend with Darren in the next seventy-two hours. I avoid that particular topic. "I'll be home in a couple of hours. Grab a cab and let yourself in." I take a quick glance at my watch—6:05 p.m. We say our goodbyes and hang up.

Back in the file, property records indicate Ward owns two residential houses—one here in Los Feliz and an apartment in New York. And according to Mercedes' search of companies, Ward is on three boards, including being chairman of two of his father's original companies. Mercedes has provided copies of the short bios posted on these companies' Web sites, from which I glean that he attended private school and studied a Bachelor of Arts at Stanford University, taking courses in art, art history and history. The only thing on the police system for him is a DUI in Virginia shortly after his parents died. He lost his license for six months and has kept his nose clean since.

Looks like he moved to L.A. in 2001, a year and a half after he finished college. He has kept some of the family businesses running, but seems to mostly live off investments. Then again, it can't be too hard to draw a good salary from $270 million. No gun licenses or hunting and fishing licenses and nothing else in the system.

I lean back. We haven't found anything suspicious on Anton Ward, but you wouldn't expect much from a law-abiding citizen.

The *LA Weekly* article provides more of a personal insight into the man, and I reread it. Apparently he never watches television, comes from a Latvian background, and is into art, classical music, chess, fine dining and red wine. Of course, it had to be *red* wine. He spends four weeks a year in Europe and can't stand people with poor personal hygiene or who are badly dressed. Most of the article is about vampirism and After Dark, but throughout the piece these snippets of more personal information are revealed. Then again, everything he says fits an image— the image of an old-world, well-educated European male. I mean, how many American men in their thirties are into classical music, chess and red wine these days?

Five

Sunday, 7:00 p.m.

I head across to the Monte Cristo on Wilshire, the location of Ruin on Fridays and Malediction Society on Sundays. The bar itself doesn't open until 10:00 p.m., but hopefully there'll be someone there, setting up the club. It's 7:00 p.m. by the time I arrive, spot Sloan and get a parking spot. It takes us another fifteen minutes to find the entrance, which is down a laneway, despite the club's official address being Wilshire. The place is all shut up but we pound on the big metal door nevertheless.

"Nice neighborhood," Sloan says sarcastically. The outside of the Monte Cristo and the surrounding area is certainly nothing to brag about, but maybe that fits in with the Gothic scene.

Three posters are plastered on the door: one for Cherry Pie on Thursdays, a lesbian night; one for Ruin on Fridays; and one for tonight. A few event-specific posters are also up, such as the next full-moon party. Looks like we've come to the right place.

We bang on the door again and keep at it until eventually someone opens it a crack.

"What?" A woman comes partially into view. Even

with only a sliver of her face and body visible, I can make out legs and long black hair.

I hold up my FBI ID. "I'm Special Agent Sophie Anderson from the FBI and this is Detective Sloan from the LAPD." Sloan also holds her badge up to the crack in the door while I continue. "We'd like to talk to you about the Gothic and vampire communities here in L.A. and about some of your patrons."

The door opens fully. "Sorry. I didn't realize you were cops." The annoyance in her voice is gone. "Can we talk while I work? I'm running behind. I've got to finish setting up and get home to tuck my little girl in."

"Sure."

Sloan and I follow her in.

"Are you the manager here?" I ask.

She snorts. "No. But I do most of his work." She turns around. "I'm the bar manager, Cheryl."

Cheryl's tall, at about six-two, although a few inches of that is high-heeled boots that come up to her thighs. She wears skimpy black hot pants and a burgundy bodice, strapped tight. Her dark black hair is long and straight, with a heavy fringe.

"Are you a vampire, Cheryl?" I ask.

She shakes her head. "Nope. And personally I think it's all crap. But we get lots of people in here who think they are vamps."

"After Dark?" Sloan is struggling to keep up with Cheryl's strides.

"Sure. Most of them come in here—if not every Friday and Sunday at least a couple of times a month. Including their leader, Anton Ward."

"You know how many people are in the group?"

She shrugs. "There's about twenty in Ward's house."

"House?"

"Coven, house, clan. It's what they call themselves."

Cheryl ducks under the side of the bar. "You ladies want a drink? On the house of course."

"Water, if you've got it."

She smiles. "Guess you're still on duty, huh?"

"Yeah." Sloan lets out an exaggerated sigh. "I'll have a water, too."

"Two waters coming up." Cheryl bends down into a fridge directly beneath her and places two bottled waters on the bar. Sitting on the bar stools, Sloan and I open the drinks.

"Are there lots of vampire houses?"

"Sure." Cheryl pauses, looking around the bar. "Sugar syrup." She grabs a bag of sugar and pours some into a jug, and then takes out a kettle and plugs it in. "I guess there's about four bigger houses that I know of for sure. But even two or three vamps just hanging out might call themselves a house."

"You got any names?" Sloan leans forward in anticipation.

She shakes her head. "The others are small fry compared to Anton's house. After Dark's the most well-known because of its elite nature."

"So tell us about Ward." I take a sip of water.

Cheryl starts cutting lemons. "His group's been around for ages...longer than I've been here."

"How long *have* you worked here?" Sloan asks.

"Four years."

"That's a long time," I say in between mouthfuls of water.

"Yeah. For this place and bar work in general. But it suits me. I live down the road and can pop back home to say good-night to my little girl, and the tips are good. And the boss...well, I know I said before he should be here, but I like it that he's not on my back all the time." She shrugs. "No reason to move on."

"So four years ago..." Sloan takes a quick glance

around the room. "Ward and After Dark much as it is now?"

"Uh-huh. Maybe a few more members, but that house is pretty stable."

"Good leadership?" I ask.

"Guess so. Ward's certainly...charming. And good-looking." She stops chopping lemons for a second and looks up. "There's something about him, he's got...what's that French expression?"

"Je ne sais quoi?"

"That's the one." She gives us a wink. "A great ass, too."

"Sounds like you're smitten." Sloan smiles.

"No." She shakes her head. "He's not my type. Way too sure of himself. I like my men a little more submissive." Another wink.

The kettle clicks off and she pours the boiling water into the jug and stirs while she talks. "But lots of women do like him. He's got a few from his clan, of course, plus...well, pretty much any woman who comes in here would jump at the chance to get into bed with Ward."

"I see." I'm getting curious now. I know from the photos that he's good-looking, model good-looking, but obviously there's more to it than that. Then again, as the leader of a large group, cult or not, he's bound to have a charismatic and magnetic personality.

"Many people leave After Dark?" I ask.

"No, not really. Like I said, it's a stable house. And Ward's wealthy, real wealthy, so I think the members get lots of fringe benefits."

"Such as?" Sloan stands up and for the first time today gets out her notebook, pen and reading glasses.

"I don't know for sure, but I've heard he buys them clothes and jewelry, plus he's got a standing tab here for drinks. And I think the group meets at his house once a week and the whole thing's catered." She stops stirring the sugar syrup and puts it in the fridge before moving back to the last two whole lemons.

I watch her making quick, exact slices. "Does it cost money to become a member?"

"I don't know." She pulls out a basket of limes and a few cartons of strawberries.

"Anyone left After Dark recently?"

"Yeah, actually. Damien Winters. Used to be close to Ward, too, but he broke off a little bit ago." She cuts the limes into quarters. "He hangs out with a different bunch of people now."

"What's Damien Winters like?"

She shrugs. "He's okay. Both he and Ward have very strong personalities and I presume that's why he left—a house with two alpha males just doesn't work."

Sloan stops scribbling and looks up. "Either of them ever violent?"

"Not that I know of."

"You know who's in Winters' group?"

"There are twin brothers from Texas. Real thick Texan accents, and *they* are rough." She finishes the limes and moves onto the strawberries, cutting little slits in them. Presumably they'll be decoration for cocktails tonight. "Security always keeps a close eye on them. And there are a few girls who hang around Winters, too. Don't know their names, but I assume they're girlfriends or donors."

"Donors?"

"The ones who like having their blood drunk by vamps."

Sloan grimaces. "The vamps that come in here, are they more about the look, or do they really believe they're vampires?"

"There's some that have this romanticized idea of the Goth culture and think vampires are sexy...cool. But there are lots of true believers, too, including After Dark. And you don't want to question their beliefs. I learned a long time ago to keep my mouth shut on the subject."

"They get angry?"

"Not angry, defensive." She looks up. "You walk down the street like this and you get looks, you can get picked on. Vamps often feel persecuted. Most of them believe they were born vampires, with some sort of need for blood, and that nobody understands that. Nobody but other vamps."

I nod. "What about the other houses in L.A.?"

"Like I said, even two vamps who are friends can call themselves a house."

"You must have some names? Some records?"

"Credit card receipts, I guess. And we've got a mailing list and a few of our members have bar tabs. But you'll have to talk to the manager about that."

Fair enough. Realistically we'd need a warrant for that information anyway.

"There's also our MySpace and Facebook pages. Most of the friends on there are regulars."

"I was on the club's pages this afternoon, but I'll take a closer look. Thanks." I take a final sip of water. "Any of your other customers ever violent or dangerous?"

"Mmm...there's one guy that gives me the creeps. Don't know his name, but he's big and always seems real aggressive—even just in the way he demands a drink. He's always here with his girlfriend and two other guys. I don't know if they're a clan or just hang together." She finishes the strawberries and stretches up to take a small blackboard on the bar's corner off its hinges. "I've heard they're really into the whole mythology. And that they're convinced they must feed off people and turn them to increase their vamp numbers. But it could all be talk."

"And you don't know any of their names?" Sloan asks.

"Sorry, no." Cheryl writes: *Cocktail special: Deadly*

surprise, *$12* on the blackboard and rehangs it before moving down to the other end of the bar and taking another small blackboard off its hinges, then returns to the center of the bar. "They usually come in on Sundays, though. I could point them out to you…" Midsentence she looks up and gives us a big smile. "You ladies got any black?" She looks back down at the board and writes in the drink special.

"Can you describe them to us?" I won't be mentioning that I'm considering coming back tonight. I'm not sure if I want Cheryl, or anyone, knowing that I'm FBI here in disguise. And with the makeup, the clothes and a wig, I don't think Cheryl would recognize me anyway. I grimace at the thought of me in Goth gear. All in the line of duty.

"The main guy is around five-ten, stocky and bald with a big skull tattoo on his right arm. He usually wears leather pants and a fishnet-T. The girlfriend is big, buxom. Long black hair with bright red streaks and she's always showing a lot of flesh…and she's got a lot to show. Then the two guys…one of them is real tall and skinny, hair down to his shoulders and he normally wears full face makeup and a suit. Think *Clockwork Orange.* And the other guy is kinda short, maybe five-six, but good-looking in a rough kinda way. Short black hair, not much makeup, and he goes more for the leather pants and usually nothing on top. Two nipple rings and a nose stud, too."

I nod. "Thanks, Cheryl."

Sloan closes her notebook. "It's been enlightening, ma'am."

Cheryl gives a little laugh. "Thanks." She pauses. "We're done?"

Sloan and I both say yes.

Cheryl wipes her hands on a tea towel. "I'll let you out then."

We follow her back through the club to the main entrance.

"Have you got cameras in here?" Sloan's scanning the ceiling.

"Uh-huh." Cheryl stops and points backward. "One in the corner there, one on the rooftop patio and one at the entrance."

"Do you know if the manager keeps the footage?" Maybe we can find the four people Cheryl's talking about on video footage.

"Yeah, I think so. But I don't know for how long. I can write down the manager's contact details for you. There's a pen at the door." She starts walking to the entrance again.

"Great," Sloan says.

We get to the top of the stairs and follow Cheryl down. "I like your top."

"Yeah, it's cool isn't it?" She looks back at me and gives me a once-over. "You could wear something like this with black pants and it'd look dressy, not Goth, right?"

"True. Where'd you get it?"

She goes behind the desk at the door and pulls out a pen and paper. "Place called VampIt in WestHo." She starts writing. "So the manager's name is Brad and he organizes all the security."

I take the piece of paper. "Thanks."

"No problem." She unlocks the heavy metal door and heaves it open.

"Thanks again for your time." Sloan holds out her hand.

Cheryl smiles and takes Sloan's outstretched hand, then mine. "Have a good night."

It didn't take me long to track down VampIt and recruit

Mercedes for the night's activities. I'm bringing her along as a friend, not as an FBI employee. Not many women go to a club by themselves and I don't want to stand out. Mercedes and I met at the store in WestHo, leaving Sloan to catch a cab back to her house. I got the distinct impression she didn't see the point of actually going to one of the clubs in Goth attire at this early stage of the investigation, but if I'm going to profile Sherry's killer I need to look at all angles.

It had actually been kinda fun shopping for corsets, leather and black. Mercedes and I spent a good forty minutes in the shop, much to the annoyance of the sales-girl who agreed to keep the store open for us when we guaranteed her sales and a big tip…but after twenty-five minutes I think she was regretting her decision. Even creatures of the night want to knock off work. We were lucky the store was even open.

Eventually I chose black leather pants with laces that run all the way up the sides of my legs and a red velvet bodice top—one of the few in the store that had straps. Rather than wasting money on shoes, I decided to wear some ankle boots I had at home, but I did buy an ankh choker, which is supposed to represent eternal life. Mer-cedes' outfit is very different from mine. She chose a short black leather dress with an A-line flare to it and a halter neck. She also managed to pick a pair of knee-high boots that she figured would work well in her normal wardrobe, some fishnet stockings, plus a long chain and chunky pendant. The last things on our shopping list were makeup and wigs. The shop assistant suggested going a few shades paler than our own skin tones in the founda-tion, and then purchasing a translucent powder. Despite my stereotyped notion that I'd be going for white, appar-ently that's considered a bad makeup job among Goths. Who knew?

I'm already pretty pale, especially by L.A. standards,

so I go with Ivory Bisque for the foundation. But for Mercedes, whose Latin-American blood gives her a beautiful olive tone, the shop assistant recommended Light Beige Blush. We also bought one container of "ash" powder, an almost translucent powder that will set the makeup and our respective foundations, only making the overall effect slightly paler. The piece de resistance was two wigs. Mercedes went for an Uma Thurman in *Pulp Fiction* look, and I decided on a long black do with no bangs. I reckon it was worth the sales assistant's forty minutes, because the bill totaled $655 and we gave her a $40 cash tip for her efforts. Goth clothes are expensive and I don't know yet if the FBI will let us write them off. Truth be told, it's a big investment, but I need to find out more about the vampire community. The more I know, the better informed my profile will be.

By the time Mercedes and I get back to my Westwood apartment it's 8:30 p.m. and I can't imagine Darren's exactly happy with me. I called from VampIt to scrap our dinner plans but I had a hard time convincing Darren that this little outing was important and couldn't wait.

I slide my key in the door and creep in sheepishly, Mercedes in tow. The television's on and Darren's sitting on the couch with a beer in hand. On the kitchen counter are several takeout containers.

"I'm really sorry about dinner," I say, straight off the bat.

Darren stands up. "Hey, Soph." He comes over and gives me a kiss on the cheek. Not exactly our usual first kiss, but then again Mercedes is standing right next to me.

"Hi, Mercedes. Nice to see you again."

Mercedes smiles. "Hi, Darren."

"I saved you guys some Chinese. I presume you haven't eaten?" It's only half a question, because Darren knows what I'm like when I'm on a case—I often forget to eat.

"Thanks."

"I'd love some," Mercedes says. "We got time?"

"Sure. A quick bite." I know it'll take us a while to get dressed and put on the makeup, but we do need to eat.

Darren and Mercedes lean on the living room side of the kitchen counter while I get out two bowls and place a few spoonfuls of rice in each one. "Beef in black bean sauce or shrimp and vegetables?"

"I'll take the beef, thanks."

I spoon most of what's left of the beef into Mercedes' bowl and fill mine up with the prawns.

Darren grabs his beer from the coffee table and sits at the small dining table. At least he's sitting down with us.

"You want some more?" I ask.

He shakes his head. "I'm done."

As soon as we're seated, Darren takes a deep breath. "You really have to go tonight?"

"Yes." I stick to my guns. "There are only four Goth nights a week around town—Thursday, Friday, Saturday and Sunday nights. And it can't wait until Thursday."

He hesitates, but doesn't stop himself. "Can't wait, or *won't* wait?"

Mercedes, head down, is pretending not to notice the start of a potential fight.

I give Darren a forced smile. "Let's talk about it later." I glance at Mercedes and he gives a reluctant nod. He knows it's out of line to start *that* conversation when we're not alone.

"So tell me about the club." His tone is much lighter.

"Don't know much about it yet. It's a nightclub near downtown that has two Goth nights and one lesbian night. Guess we'll know more in a couple of hours."

Darren nods. "And I see you've got a shopping bag there." He gives a little raise of the eyebrows. "Can't wait to see the outfits." The Darren I like…maybe love… returns.

Once we've finished eating, we start the transformation in my bedroom, leaving Darren to channel-surf in the living room.

"Looks like you're in trouble," Mercedes whispers.

"It's not exactly the best start to our few days together, but it can't be helped."

"Are you sure about that? Why don't we just wait until Thursday?"

"Darren will cope. Besides, I need to get on top of this angle ASAP. I get the feeling the lead detective isn't too sure about her decision to call in the Bureau."

"And you want to prove yourself?" She frowns.

"Not prove myself…I just want to be thorough."

Mercedes rolls her eyes. "You're always thorough."

"My job's important to me." I sound defensive, but I can't help it.

"I know." Mercedes puts her hand on mine. "But you need a life outside of the job. And Darren…he's a good guy."

I sigh. "You're right. I need to get better at the whole balance thing." Generally speaking, if I'm not working I'm exercising, and vice versa. And my kung fu takes up a big chunk of time each week too, especially now that I'm working toward my second dan black belt. "This will only take us a few hours and Darren will be fine." I don't know if I'm convincing Mercedes or myself.

Mercedes takes the leather pants I bought out of the VampIt bag. "Most men would forgive anything if they saw their girl in this outfit." She gives me a big smile and passes the pants to me.

"Good." I lay my clothes out on the bed and Mercedes does the same. Looking at the clothes makes me feel like a teenager dressing up for a nightclub or a high school dance. "We need music."

"I don't have anything Goth in my music collection. You?" Mercedes is in her underwear and we both stand at my full-length mirror about to start our makeup.

"I used to listen to Madonna when I was getting ready in my teens."

She shrugs. "I'm up for Madonna. But I don't think it would help us get into character."

I laugh. "Let's see how we go without any mood music then."

We both start with regular moisturizer before applying the base, smoothing it over our faces and necks.

I check out Mercedes. "That looks nice." She's definitely a few shades paler than normal, but doesn't look like she's putting on a clown face, either. I take my dressing gown off and mix the foundation with regular moisturizer to tone it down. My arms and décolletage are already pale and won't need much work, but I want to blend the effect across my upper body, given I'll be wearing a corset. Once I've smoothed the blend over my arms and chest, I use the ash powder to dust my face, arms and chest. It creates an even, velvetlike finish and, just like the girl said, it only lightens the tone of the base by one or two shades.

I pass the powder to Mercedes. "Knock yourself out."

"Thanks." Mercedes looks at her reflection. "Man, how do you stand being this pale all the time?"

I give her a light push. "Don't get me started. I'd trade skin tones any day." Mercedes' skin is beautifully smooth and olive. No need for fake tan, or solariums or even a body bronzer.

She smiles. "Pity you're not really a Goth."

When I'm done, my face, décolletage and arms are Nicole Kidman pale. Mercedes, on the other hand, looks more like my natural skin tone but it's still enough to give a Goth pallor, especially once we add dark eye shadow and lipstick.

We move onto our eyes next. Again, we follow the shop assistant's suggestions of using liquid eyeliner underneath and on top of our eyes. I hardly ever wear much makeup, so I borrow Mercedes' and need her help drawing the thin lines and then smudging them slightly.

Mercedes takes a step back and looks at her handiwork. "You should go for dark gray eye shadow. And I'll use dark brown."

"Okay."

She passes me an open compact. "Try this one." She points to a coal-gray.

"That's almost *black*."

She puts a hand on her hip. "We *are* going Goth."

"Sorry, you're right."

While Mercedes puts on her eyeliner, I start on the eye shadow, smoothing the rich color onto my eyelid.

A couple of minutes later, Mercedes' eyes are highlighted with dark brown, and mine with gray. The look is striking.

"Good job." Mercedes looks at our reflections in the mirror. "Okay, lipstick."

We each bought dark red lipsticks, but Mercedes' has a little more plum in it. Again, the redness will accentuate my white skin and blue eyes, and the plum-red will contrast against Mercedes' skin tone and deliciously dark eyes.

With our lipstick on, we both take a few steps back from the mirror.

"I think we're done with the makeup."

I look at my watch. "Let's get dressed and head over." I grab the leather pants and wiggle into them. The size up was too big, too loose, but I can barely squeeze myself into the U.S. size four.

"They look really hot, Soph."

I laugh. "Thanks. If they didn't have the lacing that shows off flesh at the side, I might even wear them out normally."

"You could just tighten that. Then you wouldn't be flashing anything." She takes the dress out of the bag and steps into it.

"Tighten?" I run my hands along my hips and raise my eyebrows. "You think these pants should be *tighter?*"

Mercedes laughs. "They're not that bad. Besides, you've got the figure for it." She turns her back to me so I can zip her dress.

With the dress done up, she looks in the mirror and gives herself a wink. "Smoking." Mercedes does a half turn and looks at her back in the dress. "My ass doesn't even look big in this. Gotta love an A-line." She pulls on the knee-high boots, with laces all the way down the front and a zip on the inside.

"You are smoking." I smile.

"It's very different to my normal look, that's for sure." She blows out a forceful sigh. "Thank goodness John won't see me in this get-up."

"I can take photos now and you can tease him with them."

"Pass."

Photos… "Actually, when I'm finished I might get you to take a pic. If I look different enough to Sophie Anderson I can use it for a fake profile for Facebook and MySpace."

I slip my arms into the slight sleeve of the corset and position it on my boobs, before reaching around to zip it up.

Mercedes motions with her finger for me to spin around and I let her force the zipper up. It would actually be a real struggle to do it myself, especially with fake corset laces running on either side of the zipper.

"My guess is Darren will be waiting up for you to-night and all will be forgiven." She laughs.

"Ha, ha." I pause, still looking in the mirror. "I hope you're right." I bite my lip. "Time for our wigs."

"Ah—" Mercedes grabs the two wigs out of the shop-ping bag "—how could we forget?" She passes me the longer wig.

It takes a little positioning, but eventually I get it sit-ting correctly. Mercedes could have foregone the wig, but we both agreed she should look different enough that people wouldn't easily recognize her, if at all. I, on the other hand, didn't have an option. Blond hair in a Goth nightclub—I don't think so.

Once my boots are on, I check out the full effect in the mirror. I definitely look chic Goth—mission accom-plished. And I look nothing like me, nothing like Special Agent Sophie Anderson.

"It'd be fun to walk into the office like this…see if anyone recognized us." Mercedes has a glint in her eye.

"We'd never live it down." I look at myself in the mirror one more time. "Not much room for a gun." In fact, there's nowhere to conceal my gun so I decide to take a handbag big enough for my Smith & Wesson 9 mm.

"Ready?" Mercedes asks.

"Yup. Time to get our first reaction." I sling my hand-bag over my shoulder and lead the way.

Darren turns around as soon as he hears the door open-ing and his jaw drops. "Holy cow."

I smile. "Pretty intense, huh?"

"You look…great." He stands up. "Hot, of course, and very, very Goth." He looks past me to Mercedes. "You, too, Mercedes."

"Thanks." Mercedes looks at Darren then me. "I'll pull the car around. See you out front?"

"Sure."

"Don't be too long." She gives me a wink

As soon as Mercedes is out the door, Darren pulls me in for a kiss and his hands quickly travel down my waist and to my butt. Maybe he *will* forgive me.

"That's some ass."

I smile. "Genetics and squats…a magic combination."

He laughs and gives me another kiss. Eventually the kiss ends and he says, "Sure I can't come tonight?"

I take a step back and give Darren a look up and down. "Can't imagine you in the clothes, to be honest." Darren is what I would call clean-cut American. Jeans and a T-shirt or a leather jacket is pretty much the extent of his wardrobe.

"Maybe you're right. Looks good on you, though." He pulls me in again, but I push him away.

I smile. "No way am I risking another kiss. Not when Mercedes is waiting." I swivel on the ball of my foot and let him watch the rear-end show. "Don't wait up for me, honey."

"I am *so* waiting up."

On the way over I let Mercedes drive, while I do some online research on my BlackBerry. Today I pretty much guessed from the context what Cheryl meant by "house" and "donor," but I'm sure the vamp community has a whole slew of its own slang. And given we're supposed to be part of that group, it'll look pretty silly if we can't speak the lingo.

"I've got something," I say as Mercedes merges on the I-5, southbound.

"Shoot."

Not surprisingly I got loads of hits when I searched on "vampire terminology" and after scanning the first few results, I opt for the fourth entry, which seems to be the most comprehensive.

"Okay, let's start with the A's. *Auto-vampirism,* when you drink your own blood."

"Eew."

"Yeah."

"*Awakening*…it says here that vampires are usually awakened around puberty. That's when they start craving blood, feeling sensitive to light and moving to a nocturnal lifestyle."

"O-kayyyyy."

"*Beacon*…apparently vamps have some sort of beacon to attract other vampires…" I keep reading. "Oh, this is funny. Under beacon it also mentions the word *vampdar.* It's like gaydar…but a vampire radar."

Mercedes laughs.

I keep scanning through the Web page. There's no way we can learn all of these terms in the fifteen to twenty minutes it will take us to get to the club at this time of night, so I look for ones that I imagine would be more common in everyday speech or when first meeting other vampires.

"*Blood junkie*…someone who has no control over their blood thirst." I move on to the next one. "Here's another play on words from the gay community. "*Coming out*… of the coffin."

Mercedes laughs again. "Yup, like that one, too."

"*Donor*…someone who gives their blood to a vampire." I scroll down to the *F's.* "*Feeding,* i.e. drinking blood. *H, the hunger,* also known as the thirst or need…means the need to feed."

Mercedes takes the exit onto I-10, traveling east.

I keep scanning through the alphabet, but it's not until I get to *P* that I find something interesting—*Psychic vampires.* My initial reaction is to roll my eyes and comment on how pathetic it sounds…except that I have psychic visions.

"According to this there are two types of vampires—

psychic vampires who drain your life energy rather than blood, and then the vampires who feed on actual blood." I scan the entry further. "And some vamps can do both."

"There are a few people at work who suck the life force out of me."

I laugh. "Gonna name names?"

"No." She shakes her head.

I keep moving through the alphabet. "A rogue, which is either a donor who parted company with his or her vamp on hostile terms, or a vampire who becomes violent and irresponsible. Maybe the group I told you the bar manager mentioned today are rogues within their community. It sounded like they were pretty rough."

"And you want to find these people?"

"At some stage, yeah. But that's not what tonight is about. Tonight I just want to get a feel for the vamp community."

Mercedes nods. "I can help you tomorrow with all the social-networking stuff. Once you're online with some of these people you'll get a good idea of the personality types, too."

"Thanks."

Next in the *R's* is *Renfield's syndrome,* a psychological condition that "explains" vampirism. I read it with interest, but it's something I'll revisit more closely tomorrow. There are a few terms derived from *sanguine* and *blood,* and the next *S* is *sexual vampirism.* "You'll like this one," I say to Mercedes. "*Sexual vampirism*…feeding on sexual energy."

"As in during sex?"

"Um, it says here that it can be someone's sexual energy or the energy generated during sex. So both, I guess."

Mercedes looks down at her leather dress. "Maybe that's partly why they wear these clothes. I mean, it's not my taste but it is damn sexy. I even *feel* sexy. And if they think they can feed off that vibe…" Mercedes takes us off the freeway and onto Vermont Avenue.

"True." I move back to my BlackBerry screen and the glossary. "*Vampire bait*…someone who wants a vampire to bite them. It also says *vampire bait* is a *wannabe*. And *wannabe* is the last term here. Pretty self-explanatory… it's someone who wants to become a vampire but isn't one."

"Maybe that's all we're going to look like tonight. Wannabes." Mercedes keeps driving north, heading back up to Wilshire.

"Surely our age will be on our side. Maybe I'm wrong, but I envisage wannabes as teenagers. You know, kids who are fans of all the vampire movies and books and just want to be a part of it."

"We're gonna look real old in there, aren't we?"

"No. I checked out the club online and the photos show different ages up to about forty." I pause. "And Anton Ward, the leader of After Dark, is in his thirties."

Mercedes nods. "Okay, I feel better now." She looks down at herself again.

I laugh. "You're worried we're mutton dressed as lamb?"

"What?"

"Oh…sorry, it must be an Australian expression." I'm starting to lose track of what expressions are Australian and which ones are American—guess I have been surrounded by Americans for nearly two years now. "Mutton dressed as lamb means an older woman dressed in something that's more suitable to someone much, much younger."

"God, that's us."

I shake my head. "We're way too hot to be mutton."

We both laugh.

Six

We get a parking spot a block and a half away and both feel more than a little exposed as we walk to the club. Just before we left the car I took another look at the photos I have of Anton Ward and Damien Winters. The only pic of Winters is from his driver's license, but hopefully it will be enough for me to recognize him.

It's 10:20 p.m. by the time we're walking down the alley to Monte Cristo and Malediction Society. The place still looks a little rough from the outside, but small candles run the length of the laneway and instantly give the venue character.

It's been a long time since I've been on the club scene and I feel like an excited teenager. I'm sure the dress-ups are adding to the thrill, and I have to admit I'm more than a little intrigued by Anton Ward. But I remind myself of the real reason we're here: Sherry Taylor.

"Ladies." The doorman pulls aside a rope for us. "Come in."

"Thank you." I immerse myself in the character of Veronica, vampire and temptress. I also put on my best American accent.

After paying the club's entrance fee, we walk up the flight of stairs and the thumping of the music gets louder. "The music's terrible," I say to Mercedes.

She nods. "And imagine how much worse it will be when we're up there."

I grimace. "Maybe we are mutton."

Mercedes laughs and we take the last few stairs. The place looks different than it did a few hours ago, when full lighting showed up scuffed floors and stained upholstery. Now colored lights flow over the bar and dance floor, and the chandelier and a few high wall-mounted candles create a definite ambience. The furniture that looked drab earlier now looks inviting and even somehow romantic. Behind the bar, three pink lights reflect off the white plaster, creating a textured effect. I can see Cheryl making a cocktail, and one other barman helps her serve. The bar's busy, but it's probably just the first rush of the evening. There are only about sixty people here; still early for a club.

Mercedes leans into me. "Want a drink?"

"Yeah. Do you mind getting them? I don't want the bar manager to see me."

"There's no way she's going to recognize you, but I'll get the drinks. Beer?"

"Yeah, I'll have a Beck's."

"Sure."

I sit down on a corner couch that faces outward—the perfect place to people-watch.

Nearly ten minutes later, Mercedes hands me my bottle of Beck's.

"Cheers," she says and we clink our bottles together. "Seen anyone interesting?" Mercedes takes a seat next to me.

"*Interesting* is not a problem, but no sign of Anton Ward or Damien Winters. And I haven't seen anyone who matches the descriptions of the rogue vamps, either."

Mercedes nods. "You wanna move? Apparently there's a rooftop patio through that door."

I look around the room. "Let's hang out here for a bit. The place is only just getting started anyway."

We spend the next hour observing the scene. Fashions range from a more Goth-punk look to the romanticized Victorian, and there are certainly women showing a lot more flesh than us, including some in only bodices, fishnets, knickers and suspenders. Although I've been keeping my eye on the door on and off, I've either missed my targets or they haven't arrived. Given I've been looking around quite a bit and could have easily missed our targets' entrance, I decide it's time to move. Besides, I've been nursing the same Beck's for an hour now and it's time for another drink.

I lean into Mercedes and yell in her ear. "Come on. Let's take a look around."

"Thank goodness. My legs are falling asleep."

"What, you want to dance?"

She laughs. "Not to this."

We're moving toward the bar when I notice several heads turning. Mercedes and I instinctively follow suit and see Anton Ward, flanked by two women, standing at the top of the stairs. The threesome moves forward, with another three couples in tow. Just like everyone else in the room, I feel myself drawn to them, to him.

Ward certainly is striking. He's six foot, maybe six-one, with a slim build, and his coal-black hair looks sculptured, like every strand has been meticulously placed to frame his face and the nape of his neck in a feathered, almost feminine manner. His pearly whites are just that— whiter than white with a pearl-like sheen—and even from here his skin looks silky and pale. His clothes are an unusual juxtaposition of modern and historical. A white shirt has a slight flare at the sleeves and is tucked into tailored black pants that taper at the bottom, following the natural line of his leg. He also wears a black velvet vest with red, black and gold brocade, and the tight vest accentuates a slim waistline and the billows of his white silk shirt. The outfit is tailored and he wears it well—he looks like he's just walked off the catwalk. There's no doubt about it, Anton Ward is hot.

"Wow." Mercedes lets out a gush of air.

"That's our guy. Keep your cool."

She looks at me and raises her eyebrows. "Keep *my* cool." She leans in. "You could lose the dropped jaw, honey."

I laugh. "Okay, okay."

She looks back at Ward and shakes her head. "Of course *he's* the one you're after."

Ward scans the room, taking the clubbers in like mere peasants to his aristocracy. His eyes seem to rest on me for an extra beat, before moving on to Mercedes and then to the people nearest us. The whole lackadaisical look only takes him five seconds, but I get the feeling he's soaked up everyone in the room in that short time frame. Just like a cop or FBI agent would. And why did his eyes linger on me? Do Mercedes and I stick out in some way?

Ward moves, and his entourage follows. Presumably they're all After Dark members, but it's impossible to know for sure. Does he have a girlfriend and friends who aren't in After Dark, or is his social life exclusive to his house? They make a beeline for the bar, and the other club-goers part down the middle so Ward and his crew can walk a straight line without having to weave through the masses. He certainly is treated like a celebrity…just what cult leaders normally expect…and demand.

There is a definite energy about him.… I know what Cheryl was talking about when she used the expression *je ne sais quoi*. He obviously has a magnetic personality, not that dissimilar to our descriptions to date of Sherry.

But how deep was her interest in the Goth world and did she come in contact with Ward or After Dark?

Mercedes and I watch as Ward and his followers get drinks. No money exchanges hands, but Cheryl did say he had a tab. And likely the club gives him a few free drinks. If he's as powerful as he seems in the community, his presence in the club could be enough to draw people in—much like celebrities get comped everything because the exposure they bring will more than pay for any bar tab. It reminds me of an interview with Jim Carey I once saw. He joked that when he was trying to break into the business he had no money to pay for new clothes and eating out, and once he became famous he couldn't pay for these things no matter how hard he tried.

To my surprise, Ward suddenly comes directly toward us, drink in hand.

"Ladies," he shouts, just audible over the music. "Welcome to Malediction Society."

I smile. "Thanks." Again, I make sure I use an American accent, another layer of my fake identity.

Mercedes gives Ward a rather cheesy grin.

"Let's go onto the patio, so we can talk." Ward frees himself from his two women and links arms with Mercedes and me. He doesn't wait for a response, rather he assumes he won't meet resistance. I'm happy to oblige, for both professional and personal reasons. The more I can learn about Anton Ward in an unofficial way, the better…and the man is enticing. His group follows us.

As soon as we're outside, the oppressive nature of the music lifts, and I feel like I can breathe once more. Maybe I'm getting old.

Anton Ward takes in a big breath. "That's better. Now we can hear each other."

I smile. "Yes. Thank you."

The patio has spectacular views and I admire the bright lights of L.A.'s skyline.

Once we're at the edge of the patio, Ward unlinks our arms, turns us around and leans on the patio wall. "So, are you ladies new in town or just new to Malediction Society?"

"What gave us away?" I bat my eyelashes a little, even though I want to say: *You can't possibly know we've never been here before.*

He gives the cuffs of his shirt a quick and precise tug. "It's a pretty regular crowd in here. Same people most weeks. And I've never seen you here, or anywhere, before."

I nod. "We're new in town. This is Crystal and I'm Veronica. We just moved here from North Carolina."

"Ahh…let me guess, actresses?"

"Is it that obvious?" Mercedes gives him a flirtatious smile and a slight giggle.

I don't know the actual stats, but I'm sure at least ninety percent of the people who relocate to L.A. are actors or singers.

He holds out his hand. "I'm Anton Ward."

I take his hand, but instead of a handshake, he brings my hand up to his lips and plants a delicate kiss on it, all the while maintaining eye contact. I feel a slight tingle all over my body as his lips brush my hand. I even have to resist the urge to take a breath and let it out with a contented sigh.

Next he takes Mercedes' hand in his. "A pleasure."

She gives another little giggle and this time I'm not sure if she's playing along with our act or genuinely affected by his kiss. Who would blame her?

Ward straightens up. "And this is Teresa and Paula."

The girls both give us the slightest nods, in between their dreamy, smoldering looks. They are both beautiful, sexy women, but it seems to me they're obscured by the image they're trying to portray. Anton introduces the other three couples, but keeps his gaze firmly on me.

After a long stretch of silence, he says to me, "Your spiritual life force is very strong, Veronica." His almost-black eyes are still fixed on me. The look is hard to describe. There's something purely animalistic about his gaze—lustful, but at the same time there's almost a hint of worship in it. "I've never encountered anything quite like it," he says.

My life force? Could this somehow be related to my gift? I don't know much about people's energy or life force, but I guess it's possible that with my mind somehow linked to the future he senses something different about me.

His eyes take in my face slowly, studying every inch of it. "I am both a psi and blood vampire, and to feed on you…it would be a feast."

I try to play it cool, but am a little unnerved. "Thank you."

"You feel…different. It's most unusual, but I can't tell if you're one of us or not."

This gets the attention of his followers, who immediately seem to freeze.

Teresa moves closer to Ward. "Are you all right, master?"

He keeps his eyes on me but puts his left hand up to Teresa's face and plays with her hair. "I'm fine, Teresa. It's just…unusual."

"Yes." She leans her head into his shoulder, somewhat comforted.

Maybe the girls are on drugs. There's certainly something dreamy about them, almost like their minds are only partially in the here and now. But again, it could all be part of the image. I take a closer look at the pupils of Ward, Teresa and Paula—the three closest to me—and they all seem normal.

"So, Veronica. Given I cannot read you, you will have

to tell me." He smiles, still playing with Teresa's hair but staring intently at me. "Are you one of us?"

When Mercedes and I created our characters in the car we didn't get this far. I didn't think we'd talk to anyone, much less have this sort of conversation with Ward himself. If I say we're donors, am I effectively inviting them to bite us? I'd do a lot for my job, but offering my blood definitely crosses the line. Besides, Ward's already looking at me like I'm something between a snack and a conquest; the last thing I need is to offer myself up to him. But if we say we're vampires, will he then produce a couple of willing and able donors for us?

I lift my eyes to his. "I am, and Crystal is my donor."

He studies us closely. "You are partners?"

"Friends," I answer evenly.

There's a long moment of contemplative silence before he takes his hand away from Teresa and delicately cups my jaw. "I could feel your presence as soon as I entered the club. It's almost overwhelming." Again his eyes travel over my face as though he's searching for something. The intensity of the look and his dark eyes takes my breath away.

I try to hide the gulp, try to hide my desire to run—although I'm not sure if I'd run away from him or to him. A glance at Paula and Teresa tells me they're less than impressed that Ward's paying me so much attention.

With his face only inches from mine and his hand still resting against the length of my jaw, Ward takes a deep, long breath almost like he's drinking me in. Then he suddenly withdraws and pulls a card from his vest pocket. "I'm throwing a party tomorrow night. I'd like you… and Crystal…to come." He takes the hands of Teresa and Paula. "Until tomorrow." He gives us a nod and turns abruptly, moving back inside the club.

I let out a sigh and turn around, leaning my wobbly elbows on the patio wall.

"What was that about?" Mercedes is curious, but I also get a hint of jealousy in her tone.

"I don't know. I guess he wants my blood...my energy."

She smiles. "I think he might want more than that."

"I'm just glad we got through it." I turn around again, leaning my back against the barrier. "I'm sorry, Mercedes. I should never have brought you."

"Don't sweat it. Besides, having to think on my feet was worth it to meet him."

I bite my lip. "I know what you mean. But I put you on the spot. I didn't think we'd actually talk to him. That he'd ask all those questions. I just wanted to soak up the atmosphere tonight, observe the community in its own environment."

Mercedes puts her hand on my arm. "I know. Seriously, it's all good. Besides, we got through it."

I shudder. "He gives me the...creeps."

"Creeps? Sure didn't look that way to me. He's... divine."

"Okay, *creeps* isn't the right word. *Disturbingly alluring* might be a better way to describe it."

Mercedes is silent for a while, staring at the doorway into the main club. Eventually she says: "The scary thing is, I wanted him and that didn't disturb me one little bit."

True to his word, Darren is waiting up for me when I get home.

"How'd you go?"

"Mmm...good question." I put my keys on the kitchen counter and flop onto the sofa next to him. "I met Anton Ward."

"The leader of the group you were telling me about?"

"Uh-huh."

"And?"

"He's an interesting guy, all right." I drape my legs over Darren's lap and semi-recline on the couch. "He said he could sense something about me. That my life energy was particularly strong."

"And you don't think it was just a line?"

I screw up my face. "I don't think so. That's the problem. He was very…intense and very sure of himself."

"He's the leader of a community of vampires and extremely wealthy…wouldn't you expect confidence?"

"Yes. But this was…different. I can't explain it, but I really think he could sense something different, something spiritual about me." I prop myself up on my elbows. "Do you think it's possible?"

Darren shrugs. "Who knows? It sounds unlikely, but anything's possible, right?"

"Guess so."

Darren takes off my boots. "Now, let's see if I can get these pants off you."

I laugh. "You may need help. They're practically glued on."

"I've got time."

I guess all is forgiven indeed.

Darren runs his hands down the sides of my pants and plays with the laces and the flesh in between before moving his hands upward. He tries to slip his hand under the corset, but it's too tight. "Some women's clothes need instruction manuals."

I laugh and sit up with my back to him. "There's a zip at the back."

His hand brushes against my shoulder blades as he moves his way to the zipper and pulls it down. I stand up and pull him to standing, too, before leaning back into him and wiggling my hips against him. He lets out a little groan and pulls me even closer. Lifting my arms above my head, he takes the cue and pulls the tight corset up and over my head.

I lean back into him once again and move my hands onto his outer thighs and around to his butt. "Ten points for degree of difficulty." I rub my hands along his tight butt and pull him closer to me, while he runs kisses up my shoulder to my neck. When his hands move to my stomach and breasts, it's my turn to let out a little groan.

Eager to get him naked, I turn around and take off his polo shirt, before raking my hands along his chest and biceps. He leans into me, forcing me backward and onto the sofa, where he starts working on the leather pants.

He looks up at me and gives me a wicked smile. "They look amazing." He gives another few tugs and I wiggle, until eventually they slide down my hips, along with my underwear. He places delicate kisses up my legs, but I don't need foreplay, not tonight. I pull him upward and wrap my legs around his waist. On the way up he runs his hands along my thighs and lets his fingers linger to test the waters.

"You are ready," he says breathily at my ear, resting most of his body weight on his elbows but not actually giving me what I want.

I move my hips impatiently. "Stop teasing me."

He's playing with me now, moving himself closer to me but then moving his hips away. His kisses shift from my mouth to my ear. "Maybe *I'm* not ready."

But he doesn't give me time to respond before he's inside me. A groan of relief and pleasure washes over me and I pull him in farther. We move together rhythmically, starting off slow. I can't get close enough to him, can't get enough of him, and I wrap my arms and legs around him.

Our kisses become less tender and more urgent and several minutes later I can tell from his ragged breaths that he's close. I flip us over so I'm on top and suddenly my thoughts turn to Anton Ward. The fantasy is both disturbing and arousing. I dig my nails into Darren's skin and a few seconds later he comes, followed closely by me.

Seven

I arrive at our offices on the corner of Wilshire Boulevard and Veteran Avenue much later than usual. I haven't had nearly enough sleep, but then again I'm not normally out clubbing on a Sunday night.

The building is set back about three hundred feet from both roads; and the surrounding lawns, landscaped gardens and a large visitor car park give the Federal Building a sense of space, a rare thing so close to downtown L.A. As I pass through the turnstiles I give the security guard a nod and watch her direct a visitor through the metal detector. The building's entrance is separated into two sections—public to the right and employees on the left. While visitors must go through a full security check, including unloading their bags and pockets for the X-ray machine, employees simply swipe their ID card to activate the turnstiles. However, a much more intensive security system stands between the lobby and the secure levels.

Today, I've hit the building during one of its slower times, so at least I don't have to wait my turn for access. I move to the nearest "pod" and swipe my card. The pod opens and once I'm inside the door closes behind me. Next I type in my password, which opens the front of the pod and spits me into the secure foyer toward elevators that access levels eleven to twenty. On the twelfth floor I weave my way through the open-plan offices, saying good morning to Melissa as I approach her desk.

She looks up and gives me a smile. "Hey. You're in late."

I lean on Melissa's desk, noticing that Brady, the assistant director of the L.A. Field Office, is at his desk, head down. "I've got a new case. It's a really unusual one."

"You sworn to secrecy or can you spill the beans?"

"Seen the news recently?" The local stations had started reporting the discovery of a body in Temescal Gateway Park around midday yesterday. Today, Sherry's name will be released, but we'll keep the puncture marks to ourselves.

"Sure," Melissa says.

"I'm working the homicide in Temescal Park."

"Really?" She looks at me. "So it's not just a regular homicide." Melissa knows that the FBI, and my services, wouldn't be called in for a run-of-the-mill murder. Just like I did when I got the call yesterday.

"No."

She nods but doesn't press for details. Melissa likes to talk, but she knows when to keep her mouth shut. "Must have been a busy twenty-four hours," she says. "You look tired."

I instinctively put my hand up to my eyes. "And I thought I'd put enough concealer on."

"Not for a trained eye like mine."

I smile. "I was up pretty late last night."

Mercedes and I left the bar just after midnight. We probably should have stayed for longer to try to find and observe Damien Winters or our rogue four, but we were both tired…and a little unsettled by Ward. Knowing

Darren was waiting for me was also an incentive to come home.

"And I didn't sleep so well."

"Again? What's up?"

I'm not about to tell Melissa that at least a couple of nights a week I have dreams…nightmares…that seem to come and go all night, ensuring I wake up feeling like I've only had a couple of hours' sleep. And I'm certainly not going to tell her that of the dreams I manage to remember, some of them come true. Not that any of that has to do with last night. I guess I'd better buy a better concealer.

I shrug. "I'm a light sleeper."

Her eyes narrow a little.

"Seriously, I always have been."

Her concern turns to a cheeky grin. "Your man's in town, isn't he?"

I give her a smile. "As a matter of fact, yes." Although he's only partially to blame for the dark circles.

"Now that explains it." She gives me another wicked grin. "So no chic flicks tonight?"

I give a little half chuckle. "Not tonight." Although the way this case is going, Darren may have flown up for nothing.

"Melissa."

We both turn to the source of the voice—Brady.

"Yes, sir." Melissa picks up her pad and pen. "Catch you later," she says before following Brady back into his office.

I give her a wave and make my way deeper into the belly of the twelfth floor, which houses the Criminal Division of the L.A. Field Office as well as Brady, the big boss. The L.A. office has four main divisions—Counterterrorism, Criminal, the Counterintelligence and Cyber Division, and Intelligence Division. Additionally, it's got programs in white-collar crime; civil rights; and organized crime, including gang-related activities, housing one of the L.A. Safe Streets task forces. All in all, the FBI in L.A. employs 1,200 people in the L.A. headquarters and our ten resident agencies scattered across the L.A. area. The satellite offices reach from Santa Maria in the northwest to Palm Springs in the southeast corner of the FBI's L.A. territory. We cover a lot of ground, which ensures we're always busy.

While my computer boots, I look at the weekly planner that sits on my desk. It always starts off so neat, but by the end of each week a host of scribble written at various angles occupies most of the white space—names, figures, notes on autopsy results, phone numbers. On Friday afternoons I transfer unfinished things across to the next week and one of my tasks for today was to draft a presentation for the LAPD. There have been some significant changes in the LAPD's Homicide team across the city, and Brady wants me to put together a briefing targeted specifically at Homicide and what profiling services we can provide them from here, and via the Behavioral Analysis Unit in Quantico. The presentation's definitely on hold for today, but I do have four weeks until D-day. My first priority now is profiling Sherry's killer, or killers, for Sloan.

My phone's already showing a voice mail, so I dial in to pick it up.

"Hey, it's Sloan. Give me a call when you're in."

The message was left just before seven-thirty this morning.

I punch in Sloan's number and she picks up after two rings.

"Sloan." The tone is gruff.

"It's Agent Anderson."

"Hey. How'd it go last night?"

"Pretty well. I got a good feel for the club and the culture."

"Did you see Ward or Winters? Or that rogue four-some Cheryl mentioned?"

"I did run into Ward."

"Really. And?"

"I ended up talking to him."

"What?" Sloan sounds as surprised as I was when Ward walked up to us.

"Turns out the community's tight enough that Ward noticed us as newcomers."

"Damn."

"It wasn't too bad. And he did invite us to a private party at his house tonight."

"Serious?" She pauses. "I guess you should fill me in on the club and Ward, but Carey and I were just about to leave to interview Davidson and Riley." Sloan is exploring all angles, but it doesn't sound like she actually believes Ward or Riley and Davidson will lead us closer to the killer. "How's about I pick you up and we can talk in the car."

"Sure. But I better not come in for the interview."

"You met them?"

"No, but if I go to that party tonight Davidson and Riley will probably be there."

"You're seriously thinking about going?"

"Yeah, I am. Ward and After Dark might be our perps, and if not, Ward's well known in the vampire community and might be able to help."

We arrange to meet in twenty minutes on the small street that runs off Veteran and into the visitor parking. I quickly check my e-mails to make sure there's nothing urgent and decide to take my laptop and BlackBerry. Given I'll be sitting in the car while Sloan and Carey do their interview, I might as well use the time to check out a few things online, and the bigger the screen the better. I also grab a small digital recorder for Sloan to use.

Twenty minutes later I'm standing in front of the

Federal Building when Sloan and Carey pull up. I jump in the back.

"Start from the top." Sloan pulls a U-turn.

"Hey, Anderson."

"Morning, Detective Carey."

"Yeah, yeah. Morning." Sloan's not good on professional chitchat.

During the short drive to Davidson and Riley's apartment in West Hollywood I fill in Sloan and Carey, telling them everything about Malediction Society and my interaction with Anton Ward. I even tell them about his claim that I had a certain "energy" about me, figuring they'd laugh it off as bullshit. Especially if I make fun of it, too.

Sloan pulls into Poinsettia Place. "I presume you cleared it?"

"Cleared what?"

"You've made contact with a potential suspect or informant in an undercover capacity. And an undercover operation means paperwork and clearing it through the proper channels."

"Not exactly."

Sloan glances at me. "Is that a *no?*"

I hesitate, and can't help feeling like a naughty child being told off by her mother. "Yes, it's a no." I stick to my guns. "But it's not an undercover operation. I just went to the club."

"And you're talking about going to some party tonight, too."

Damn, Sloan's got me.

Carey's silent, and I'm not sure if he agrees with Sloan or just doesn't want to get caught in the crossfire.

"What if After Dark is a cult and they are murdering people?" Sloan doesn't say it with much conviction and I know she still likes the ex-boyfriend or perhaps the professor for Sherry's murder. "Don't you think you're exposing yourself, by not properly logging this investigation?"

Is Sloan right?

"And if they are involved, you're basically in. Do you know how long it would normally take an undercover operative to get into a group like After Dark? I know we don't know much about it yet, but it's a close-knit group and the fact that Ward knew you and your friend were new to L.A., to the bar…that shows how tight the community can be."

I frown, not happy with the thought of an official undercover investigation. "I'll talk to the Bureau today." I don't have much experience in the world of undercover and their assignments are often long-term. We may find evidence on Sherry's murder this week, through the autopsy or forensics, or the case could be open for months or years. I hope I haven't bitten off more than I can chew.

"Let's do this by the book, Anderson." Sloan pulls up. "This is it."

Davidson and Riley's apartment is the polar opposite of the Brentwood houses we visited yesterday. We've come from six-figure-plus salaries to double digits, from large, perfectly kept houses to a two-story apartment complex in desperate need of a paint job.

"Sit tight and we'll be back soon. I've got a good memory, so I'll give you a rundown on the conversation."

"Actually—" I pull the recorder out of my bag "—I brought this."

Sloan takes the recorder and looks it over.

"Just press that button." I point to the small red button.

She shakes her head and hands it to Carey. "I'll need my glasses to see that."

Carey lets out a hearty laugh and then stifles it when

he sees his partner's dagger eyes. "Okay." He forces a smile. "Let's go."

"Hey, before you guys go inside, where are you at with Sherry's details?"

"Credit card transactions will be through this afternoon and the same with her cell phone records. The parents said she hardly ever used the home phone, so we'll start with the cell. I've checked with UCLA, too. Sherry's acting class is scheduled for 2:00 p.m. today, so that would tie in well with our surprise visit."

I nod. "And her computer?"

"I've put a request in, but apparently the computer guys are running behind."

"Mind if I get one of the Bureau techs on it?"

Sloan looks at Carey and then shrugs. "If you think it'll speed things up, go for it."

"I'll see if anyone can move on it today."

"Sure." Sloan gets out of the car. "See you soon," she says before closing the door.

I call Mercedes directly. "Hey, are you at work?"

"Uh-huh, but tired. You?"

"Wrecked. I'm getting too old for clubbing."

Mercedes laughs. "Me, too."

"Listen, do you know if anyone there has got time to look at our vic's laptop?"

"I'll find out and get back to you."

"Thanks, Mercedes."

While Sloan and Carey are inside interviewing Riley and Davidson, I decide to search ViCAP, the Bureau's national database of violent crimes. It's possible there have been other cases of a vampire bite or puncture wounds like Sherry's. We don't know a definitive cause of death yet, so I put in the puncture marks as wounds. I get twenty-one matches, but after I sift through them it becomes obvious none were like this case, potentially linked to vampirism. I also do a keyword search with "vampire" and "vampirism" and get one match—a case from 1998 when Rod Ferrell, a self-proclaimed vampire, killed his girlfriend's parents.

I read through the case details logged on ViCAP, including the police interview with Ferrell and his confession. I also Google the case to read through the different media reports on the incident. Rod Ferrell and his gang certainly believed they were creatures of the night, but the parents were killed from blunt-force trauma—blows to the head. Nothing in the attack was carried out in a vampiric way, so it was only the group's Gothic nature and Ferrell's own claims of vampirism that linked the case in the media with the ViCAP database.

I'm still reading the last article on my computer screen when the driver-side door suddenly opens and I jump.

Sloan laughs. "What are you reading, Anderson? Something spooky?"

"Ha, ha."

Sloan and Carey climb back in the car.

"I found a vampire case in ViCAP, but it's not related to ours."

"What's the case?" Sloan asks, looking back at me.

"Rod Ferrell. Florida."

"Oh, yeah, I remember that one." She shakes her head. "Only seventeen, wasn't he? And the girlfriend watched or helped?"

"That's the one. There was some debate as to exactly what her role was." I close my laptop. "So, how'd you guys go?"

"Good." Carey passes me back my recorder.

"What did you find out?" I cue the recorder back to the beginning.

Sloan and Carey are both looking at me with big-ass smiles on their faces. They must have something.

"They recognized Sherry," Sloan says. "They think she was at Bar Sinister a couple of weeks ago."

"If she was there a couple of weeks ago, maybe Todd was telling the truth and she was there on Saturday night, too." I bite my lip. "I haven't heard back from them yet about the video footage."

Sloan starts the car. "It also confirms the link between Sherry and the Goth culture. And I'm interested enough in this angle now to interview Anton Ward."

Does this mark a turning point for Sloan? Maybe now she'll shift her focus from personal motivation to the wider vampire angle.

"We do have the puncture marks." I buckle up again.

"Yes, but I still think we need to keep an eye on Todd Fischer and check out this professor."

"Fair enough. So, Ward first and then on to Carrington's afternoon class?"

"Yup." She puts the car into Drive. "I'm looking forward to meeting this Anton Ward character. Between Riley and Davidson calling him master and acting like he's some sort of god, and your reports of him last night…"

I give a little half laugh, half snort. "And I can't wait to hear what *you* make of him."

"I guess you won't be sitting in on this interview, either."

"Sidelined again, I'm afraid." I pause, fingering the recorder. "I'm going to play this now."

"Knock yourself out." She pulls back onto Poinsettia and heads northward. "Time to see what our two-hundred-year-old vampire's got to say."

"Two hundred?" I raise my eyebrows.

"According to Riley and Davidson, their master is two hundred years old."

Carey shakes his head. "From the file we've got on this guy, he's just a spoiled rich kid who uses his charm to gather followers."

On paper, yes, but in person…

"Well, he's certainly charming." Ward unnerved me last night, mostly because I found him so seductive. And I wasn't the only one.

"He uses his charm to his advantage. But just because we can see that, doesn't mean his 'disciples' can." Sloan marks air quotes.

"I'm not a disciple or potential follower but I still found him charming." Everything about Ward is appealing— from the way he holds himself and dresses to that mysterious charisma. I'm excited by the prospect of seeing Ward again, but I'm also into the psychology behind After Dark. "Group dynamics is fascinating stuff."

"Whatever gets your motor running, Anderson."

I laugh, realizing I'd said it with a little too much enthusiasm, like a computer geek talking about code. Even though it's still unclear whether After Dark is a new religious movement or not, the prospect makes the case very interesting. And Ward's magnetism intrigues me even more.

Once I press Play, the recording starts with static, and then Sloan and Carey identifying themselves as LAPD.

"What do you want anyway?" The voice is very deep and sounds more than a little frustrated. Have the police been hounding him? It seems unlikely over a simple trespass charge. But they did investigate After Dark, so maybe Davidson and Riley got sick of questions.

"That's Davidson," Carey says and we take a right into Hollywood Boulevard.

I nod and listen as Sloan answers Davidson's question.

"We're investigating an incident over at Temescal Park."

"So naturally you thought of us."

"Something like that." Sloan pauses. "Mind if we come in and ask a few questions?"

"Do I mind? Yes. But I've got nothing to hide, so come on in."

I can hear movement as Sloan and Carey walk inside the apartment.

"So, what were you guys doing on Saturday night?" Sloan asks.

"Saturday?" It's Davidson again. "We watched *Queen of the Damned* on DVD—"

"—for the ninety-third time." The second voice is much higher in pitch than Davidson's.

"Yup, that's right," Davidson says. "Ninety-three times. And then we headed to Bar Sinister."

"Is that a Goth club?" Sloan asks, even though she knew the name from our research yesterday.

"Uh-huh."

Carey clears his throat. "So, you guys are vampires?"

"We're donors." Davidson again. Given he's more verbal than Riley, I'm thinking he's the dominant one.

"What does that mean, exactly?" Carey speaks slowly and sounds like he's genuinely interested.

Davidson answers Carey's question. "Someone who likes getting bitten by vampires."

"And you're members of Anton Ward's After Dark group?" Sloan asks.

"Yes. That's our house, our clan." This time it's Riley who responds.

"How many in the clan?"

"About twenty or so vamps plus ten donors like us." Davidson again.

"Do you meet regularly? Hold meetings?" Sloan asks.

"Sure. We usually hang out at the clubs most weeks, plus we have a special meeting once a week at the master's pad." Davidson lets out a whistle. "He's got one sweet pad."

"But he *is* immortal," Riley says. "He's had time to accrue stuff…money."

"Anton Ward is immortal?" Sloan's tone is matter-of-fact.

"Sure. He's been around for ages," Riley says. "Couple hundred years, I think. He's our master."

"He made us." Davidson's deep voice is almost somber.

"How?"

"The blood ritual."

I pause the recording. "Maybe there was another blood ritual on Saturday night and Sherry was the sacrifice."

Sloan nods. "It crossed my mind."

I press Play and Sloan's voice resonates through the speaker. "And what exactly does the blood ritual involve?"

"It's complex. And sacred." Again, Davidson's being very serious.

"Does it involve drinking blood? Human blood?"

"Of course, man," Riley says. "From a donor."

"The donors are willing? You're willing?" Sloan confirms.

"Of course." Davidson again. "No one in After Dark would ever hurt someone, or bite an unwilling participant. It's not what we're about, and Anton disapproves. We all follow the rules."

"Right on. The master's rules."

I pause the recording again. "They sound like surfies."

Sloan turns left onto N Bronson Avenue. "I know. It was bizarre."

Carey spins around in his seat fully. "Their language and demeanor was like *Bill and Ted's Excellent Adventure,* but their dress and nighttime activities sound more like…well, *Queen of the Damned*…to the ninety-third power."

I press Play again.

"Either of you know this girl?" Sloan's obviously showing them the photo of Sherry Taylor.

After a considerable pause, Riley speaks. "I think I've seen her at Bar Sinister. Made-up, you know. Dark clothes, white makeup. She looked way hotter than she does in this photo."

The photo we've chosen shows Sherry in form-fitting Antik jeans and a tight white top. The outfit shows off her figure, and her mum said it was typical of what Sherry would wear—designer jeans and a T-shirt or sweater. It's obviously not a look that appeals to Davidson and Riley.

"Where's Bar Sinister?" Sloan asks.

"Saturday nights in Cherokee Avenue."

"You only seen her there once?"

"Yeah, think so," Riley says. "She was with a black chick. But the black girl didn't quite fit in. Like she wasn't comfortable in the outfit. You know?"

"Sure. I know what you mean." Sloan's voice is reassuring. "When did you see her there?"

"Couple of weeks ago."

"What about this last Saturday night?"

"I'm not sure." Riley pauses. "The week before, though, I think she was talking to Damien."

"Really?" Davidson sounds surprised.

"Who's Damien?" Sloan asks. Again, although she knows they're probably talking about Damien Winters, she plays dumb.

There's silence for a bit before Riley responds. "We're not really supposed to talk about the dude, but he was part of our clan. Our master's right-hand man, really."

Silence.

"And?" Carey prompts.

"About three months ago the master said Damien

wasn't part of After Dark anymore," Davidson says. "And that he didn't want any of us to associate with him."

"And have you?"

"No way, man," Riley responds. "If Anton says Damien's not cool…he's off-limits."

After a few beats of silence Carey says, "Hey, I like your shoes."

"Thanks, man." '

"What size you take?"

"Eleven." Riley sounds like he thinks he's having a normal chat about his shoes.

"What size are you, Larry?"

There's a moment's hesitation. "Ten. Why?"

But neither Carey nor Sloan answer the question. Instead Sloan asks them when they were last at Temescal Park or Topanga State Park.

A long pause before Davidson finally answers. "We stay out of the parks now. We know it's illegal. Your lot charged us with trespassing and all."

"You weren't alone that night. Who else was with you?"

"Man, it's months ago. Why you on our backs again?"

"Sherry Taylor was found murdered in Temescal Park yesterday," Sloan says.

"What? No way, man." Davidson sounds shocked.

"You haven't seen it on the news?" Carey's disbelief is obvious.

"No. Besides, man, we were asleep when you came. Haven't had time to watch the news this morning yet. We're creatures of the night."

"So, were you creatures of the night near Temescal Park Saturday night?" Sloan asks impatiently.

"No. No way you pinning this on us." Davidson's voice is losing its smoothness.

"Relax, boys. We're just asking for a little help. A little cooperation."

"Yeah, right. Then you lock us up." Davidson's breathing is getting faster. "We're trying to live peaceful lives. Vampirism doesn't hurt anyone."

"Well, someone got hurt on Saturday night…someone got killed." There's silence and movement again; obviously Sloan is making a dramatic exit. "We'll be in touch, boys." The word *boys* is said condescendingly, but it sits well on a strong woman in her fifties…sits well on Sloan.

The recording finishes.

"Well?" Carey asks.

"They said Sherry was at the bar with a black girl. It's got to be Desiree."

Sloan nods. "My thoughts exactly. So why the hell didn't she tell us?" She shakes her head. "That girl's got some explaining to do."

"Agreed." I flick the ring on my little finger. "I doubt she'll be at class today, but maybe we can see her after Carrington?"

"Yup."

We're silent for a little bit before Carey lets out a sigh. "I don't get the whole biting thing. And why would anyone want to get bitten like these donors?"

"It's not that different psychologically to bondage—one person likes being the person in power, the other likes being tied up and punished."

He nods slowly. "I guess. But still, blood?"

I know what Carey means. But we see too much blood—enough for a few thousand lifetimes. And for us blood only means one thing…death.

Eight

Monday, 10:00 a.m.

While Carey and Sloan interview Ward inside his mansion, I'm sitting in the car with my laptop, researching online.

It seems there have been a number of killers over time who have been dubbed "vampire" killers because of their thirst for blood—be it literal or figurative. Although unlike Rod Ferrell, who was dubbed a vampire killer simply because of his Gothic tendencies and his claim of being a five-hundred-year-old vampire, many of the cases throughout history do involve an actual thirst for blood. As far back as 1861, a French man by the name of Martin Dumollard was draining the blood of young girls. In 1878 Italian Eusebius Pieydagnelle murdered six women and drank blood from their necks. And 1912 saw the start of Peter Kurten's reign of terror, as he raped and killed people to drink their blood. When he was interviewed he admitted he was excited by blood.

Excitement and eroticism surrounding blood is a key element in the vampire mythology—vampires are somehow perceived as sexy. However, I doubt anyone would find these killers sexy—they are simply people with an obsession for blood who have used that desire as a rationale for murder. And it hasn't been limited to men. In Santa Cruz in 1992, Deborah Finch stabbed a man twenty-seven times and then proceeded to drink his blood. And in Mexico, Magdalena Solis was part of a blood-drinking sex cult—with human sacrifices.

It's possible this last case is the most similar to ours, if our resident really did see a circle of candles. Was it a blood ritual? Some other kind of human sacrifice? Either way, it's still possible our killers have a fascination for blood without actually being active in the vampire subculture.

During my research one name keeps popping up as an expert on the subject—Jarrod Clark, a professor of Sociology at the University of Massachusetts in Boston. He's written a couple of books on America's real-life vampires and has also completed academic studies on the Goth subculture, vampire mythology and its modern-day manifestation. Sounds like he's my guy…or at least a starting point.

I call the university and ask to be put through to Clark, but introducing myself isn't quite enough to get me past his gatekeeper assistant.

"What's it regarding, please?"

"A case that I'd like his expertise on."

"One moment."

After about a minute's worth of torturous Muzak he comes on the line. "Professor Clark speaking." His voice is nasal and I'm not sure if he's got a cold or if it's his regular voice. "Agent Anderson, is it?"

"That's correct."

"How can I help you?"

"I'm working on a murder case here in L.A. that may be linked to vampires."

"Go on."

"Firstly, Professor Clark, I'd like your assurance that this conversation will be kept confidential."

He pauses for a second. "Okay."

"We're trying to keep certain case details out of the press and your cooperation is essential."

"I understand."

"Good. Yesterday morning a young woman was found murdered in a state park here in L.A. There are two definite puncture marks on her neck."

"Go on."

"We've identified a few groups, houses, of vampires in the area and we're investigating that as one line of inquiry."

"I see. What would you like to know?"

Where do I start? So many questions, so many possible angles. "First off, the bite marks. People who believe they are vampires, do they get fake teeth or something of the sort?"

"Some do, yes. Some use their existing teeth, filing their canines to a point, some get caps, while others may invest in something less permanent, usually dentures. But vampirism is more about the blood than the biting and many vamps don't feel the need for this more…cosmetic addition."

"Are these dentures or caps hard to come by?" This may be a good line of investigation for us.

"Not these days, no. Google it and you'll find a wealth of information."

I move on. "Some of the things I've read indicate that vampirism is a condition, something you're born with. What's your take on that?"

"Nearly all of the blood-drinking subjects I've interviewed indicate an overwhelming need and desire for blood. They feel they would die, or at least be very sick, without it."

"And are they?"

"Based on self-reporting, yes. Some claim if they don't have blood every day or every week, they become very ill. Common symptoms they describe include extreme lethargy, nausea, headaches and abdominal cramping."

"This ever been checked out medically?"

"Of course."

"And?"

"No underlying medical problem for these symptoms has been found."

"So it's probably psychological?"

"I believe so, yes. Although that comment would outrage many of my test subjects."

"I bet." I take a breath. "What about Renfield's syndrome? I've found some info on that online."

"Yes. So named after Dracula's insect-eating assistant, Renfield. It's a psychological disorder, which is hypothesized to start with a key childhood event that leads the sufferer to find blood exciting. Blood and this sense of excitement is later linked to sexual arousal. But I don't believe it's widely accepted in the psychological community."

I make a mental note to see what the American Psychological Association and the psychology journals have to say on the subject.

"In terms of the medical side of things, I've done a little research and read about porphyria."

"Yes, yes. A few people have proposed that the vampire mythology is based on people with the blood disorder porphyria. The disorder is treated with hemoglobin, hence the connection to drinking blood. Plus some sufferers are sensitive to light—and that gels with the vampire mythology, too. Problem is, if you drink blood it goes through the digestive tract and doesn't enter the bloodstream. It wouldn't alleviate porphyria symptoms at all." He takes a breath. "It's also been linked to rabies, particularly if you're talking about how the mythology may have started in the first place. Rabies ticks a few boxes, including hypersensitivity to light and smell, like garlic, a disturbance of normal sleep patterns, which may make the person nocturnal, and the disease can also give rise to the desire to bite others and to a bloody frothing of the mouth."

"That is a good fit."

"It's also possible people saw decomposing bodies and felt it was unnatural. I don't have to tell you, Agent Anderson, that a dead body is far from peacefully at rest. After death, gas fills the torso causing the body to swell, and blood can ooze from the nose and mouth. Industrial societies may have interpreted this as a vampire that had just fed, and was asleep in some way. After death, the skin and gums contract, making it look like the hair, nails and teeth have grown. And long nails and teeth, specifically canines, are associated with vampires."

"Sounds like a plausible explanation, too."

"Yes, although it certainly doesn't account for all the people nowadays who call themselves vampires. That's more of a cultural phenomenon."

"How many people are we talking?"

"No one knows for sure. And while there are links between self-proclaimed vampires and the Gothic subculture, not every Goth thinks they're a vampire. There are hundreds of thousands of Goths but studies show only about ten percent of Goths are vampires."

"And is there anything else that could account for a person's desire for blood?"

"There have been several medical studies on the subject, most looking at iron levels. And while iron levels in many modern-day vampires do tend to be at the lower end of the spectrum, they're usually within the normal range. Besides, if you ingest blood you don't absorb iron from it anyway."

"And what about psi-vampires?" I'm particularly interested in Clark's response to this one. Before meeting

Ward last night, I would have said it was a load of rubbish. But his reaction to me has made me curious.

"Ah, yes." For the first time the nasal monotone breaks and I can hear some amusement in his voice. "Some vampires claim to be able to feed off a person's energy. Their life force, if you will. Again, these individuals say that if they don't feed in this way they become sick and feel they would eventually die. That the hunger must be satisfied."

"But you don't believe it."

He's silent for a few seconds. "As much as some people would like to believe in vampires, my research has shown commonalities between my subjects."

"Such as?"

"Most suffer from delusions of grandeur. Claiming to be a vampire makes them feel special. Likewise, these people are often in menial jobs, but in their other lives as vampires they have control and power. After all, vampires are supposed to be strong, hard to kill and powerful— these qualities attract individuals who don't feel any of these things in their day-to-day lives."

That makes perfect sense from a psychological perspective. Certainly the psychologist in me would accept these various explanations of Clark's. But I can't dismiss Ward's attraction to me—and vice versa. It really was as though he could sense something different about me and some part of me responded to that. And surely if he simply had delusions of grandeur or this Renfield's syndrome he wouldn't pick up any vibe from me. Then again, if After Dark is an NRM and he's the leader, he could be a master conman, an expert at reading people and telling them what they want to hear—or, in my case, what I don't want to hear. If it is a farce, he probably assumes I would find it flattering.

I bring myself back to Clark. "Is it common for vampires to form houses?"

"Yes, absolutely. People with something in common are naturally drawn to one another, of course, particularly if they're in the marginal population."

"How many people are usually in a house?"

"It depends on the context, but they can range from about three to hundreds."

"And is there usually a definite leader?"

"Again, it depends on the house. Some have a group of elders and some are led by one individual."

"Would it be accurate to describe a house as a cult?"

"Interesting." He pauses. "To be honest, I don't know much about cults. What I can tell you, is that the research subjects I've interviewed all talk about a sense of community and solidarity with other members of the Goth or vampire community. To the point of feeling a bond with a stranger on the other side of the street if they're decked out in Goth clothing, too."

"Sure would make it easier to build the kinds of relationships we see in a new religious movement." I pause, thinking about other relevant questions. "And the donors, what are they like?"

"The donor nearly always has a sexual fetish for being dominated. For most vampires and donors the act of drinking blood and biting is extremely sexual. Again, I believe that's partly because of the mythology. They have been portrayed as highly sexual beings, whose desire for blood is similar to lust. I'm sure you've heard of the term 'blood lust.'"

"Yes."

He clears his throat. "In some ways vampires are the ultimate sexual fantasy for men, because a vampire can turn on women with a little *prick*." He chuckles. "A prick of the *teeth*." The joke falls a little flat. "But seriously, for many individuals in this subculture, biting or being bitten is a sexual turn-on. In fact, some of them need that as part of the sex act. A male may need it, or the prospect of biting his mate or being bitten, to get or maintain an erection. And a woman may need it to orgasm."

From a psychological perspective, vampirism is arguably a form of sexual sadism. By definition, sexual sadists derive pleasure from their partner's, or victim's, physical or psychological pain. Vampires are inflicting pain as they bite. Likewise, the donors could be seen as sadomasochists—people who need to *feel* pain to become sexually aroused or reach orgasm.

Unfortunately we're moving into a realm—sexual sadism—that I know too much about through casework. And my experiences have been extreme: serial killers who need to kill and dominate in order to become sexually aroused. The first time I heard of semen being found in a stab wound I was shocked. But now, not much shocks me. Sometimes I'd prefer to be ignorant, but most of the time my knowledge of the sick minds out there motivates me.

"Would you say vampires are dangerous, Professor Clark?"

"It depends on the individual. You're dealing with a person or persons who believe they *must* drink blood to survive. Maybe their usual session went wrong, or maybe they intentionally drained enough blood from this girl to kill her."

"It's possible it's escalation." Many criminals escalate—from robbery to armed robbery, from rape to murder. "Maybe our perps have escalated from taking small amounts of blood from their donor to taking too much. But we're talking a lot of blood."

"Studies have shown that most vampires actually only drink about a hundred milliliters of their donor's blood. And I imagine it'd take a lot more than that to kill someone."

"Yes."

"Would you like me to come to L.A.? I'd be happy to

look at your houses of vampires and offer an opinion." He gives a little sniff. "It's good research for me."

"That's very kind of you, but I'd like to keep it strictly law enforcement at the moment." We rarely bring in civilian consultants, and while I'm interested in the professor's knowledge, he doesn't need to be on the ground.

A beat of silence. "Well, let me know if you change your mind. It could be unofficial…and I'd pay for all my expenses, of course. I sure could use some warmer weather." A wheezy chuckle resonates down the phone line.

"Thanks again for the offer, but for the moment we'll keep it in-house. And I hope you feel better."

The professor is keen, but the cynic in me questions his motives. He can probably smell a book in it and I'd rather keep him away for that very reason. I thank him again for his help before hanging up.

I follow Clark's suggestion and do a quick Google search on *vampire fangs*. Crowns run at around $1,200 and dentures are about $100. And judging by the section on vampire fangs I find on one vampire Web site, there are lots of providers. Way too many to investigate.

Ten minutes later Carey and Sloan walk down the long path and get into the car.

"Well?"

"This guy's a piece of work." Carey shakes his head. "He's even got a butler."

"Really?"

Sloan sighs. "I can see the charm, I can, but he's also an egotistical prick."

Their initial response makes me feel queasy. Have I somehow been sucked in by Anton Ward? He certainly doesn't seem to have impressed Sloan or Carey.

Carey passes me back my recorder.

I focus on the psychology, not my gut reaction to Ward. "He could be delusional. He might be fooling himself as well as his members. If he believes he's two hundred years old and part of the traditional aristocracy, he'd keep a butler."

"It's very English, though, isn't it? A butler?"

I shrug. "I guess. But vampire mythology started in Europe, and European aristocracy had a similar social structure to the English. Ward is trying to project himself as the master, the lord of the house. The butler adds to that image."

"It did seem very old-world to me." Carey shakes his head again.

"Like their clothing?" I smile. "What *was* the master of the house wearing?"

Sloan chuckles. "Leather pants, a black silk shirt and this weird little corset thing."

I'm disturbed by the fact that I want to see the outfit for myself. "Loads of the guys were wearing that style at the club last night. There seemed to be two distinct looks—Goth punk, and the old-world look."

"What was he wearing last night?" Carey seems only mildly interested.

"Black pants, not leather, a white shirt and a black velvet vest with red and gold brocade."

"Nice."

"It kinda looked good, actually," I admit. "It suited him…he looked like he'd just stepped off the catwalk."

"Sounds about right." Sloan puts the car into Drive. "The autopsy was scheduled for ten, so we should get the end of it."

"Sounds good." I cue up the interview. "Don't mind me. I'll just listen to this."

The recording starts off like the last one, with Sloan introducing herself and Carey.

"I'm afraid Master Ward isn't available," a male voice says in an extremely polite manner.

"Is he home?" Sloan asks.

"Yes. But he's asleep."

"And you are?" Carey's voice has the slight disinterested tone I often pick up from him.

"Stephen French, the butler, sir."

"I think you should go wake your boss, Mr. French," Sloan says. "We're here about a murder."

A pause, then: "Right this way, ma'am, sir."

I hear footsteps echoing, like Sloan and Carey are being taken down a marble hallway with high ceilings.

I pause the recording. "What was the house like?"

"Over the top." Carey gives me a broad grin. "Antiques, but masculine, not fussy. The butler showed us into a formal living room and it even had an open fireplace and medieval suit of armor."

I think objectively about the psychology of the decor. "If Ward claims he's a wealthy two-hundred-year-old man, he would surround himself with some historical artifacts. All part of the image." I pause. "Did he claim to be two hundred?"

"Not exactly." Sloan takes a left into West Sunset Boulevard. "Keep going and you'll hear his explanation."

I press Play and the butler's voice seeps through the speakers. "If you care to wait here, I'll awaken the master. Can I offer you any refreshments? A coffee perhaps?"

"Coffee would be great. Thank you." I can hear relief in Sloan's voice. Maybe it was her first coffee for the day.

There's a stretch of silence before Carey says, "Get a load of this place."

"I know. And the butler? Puh-lease?" Sloan pauses. "Can't wait to meet Ward in person. Anderson's whet my appetite."

"Whatever." Carey sighs.

"Am I keeping you from something, Detective?" Sloan's voice is mostly humorous; so much so that I get the feeling this could be a common banter between the partners.

"Thrilled to be here."

Another pause. "I wonder if Sherry was ever here."

A door opens.

"Coffee, sir, ma'am." The voice is female this time.

I pause the recorder. "Who's that?"

"I liked her." A cheeky grin forms at the corner of Carey's mouth and I get the feeling it's for Sloan's benefit.

Sloan shakes her head. "A busty woman in a maid's uniform."

I let out a little snort. "I see." I press Play again.

"How do you take your coffee?"

"Should have seen the setup." Carey talks over the recording but I don't stop it as it's only Carey and Sloan telling the maid how they have their coffees. "Silver tray, the coffee was in a long silver pot, and there was a matching sugar bowl, cream jug and teaspoons. And the cups were fancy-looking china."

"Sounds impressive."

"Meant to impress." Sloan glances at me in the rearview mirror.

I tune back into the recorded conversation.

"Will there be anything else?" the maid asks.

"No, thanks," Sloan replies.

Silence again for a few seconds before Carey says, "Look up there."

Sloan lets out a *tsk-tsking* sound. "Now, why would Mr. Ward need to video his guests?"

I pause the recording. "A video camera?"

"Yup. Almost invisible." Carey twists around in his seat. "I only noticed it when the maid came in. When she opened the door, natural light flowed in and I caught something glistening in the bookshelf. I looked up, and there it was."

"Shit." Realization hits. "You said my name. You said 'Anderson.'"

"I thought of that, too," Sloan says. "But I didn't say your first name, or detective or agent. Besides, Ward knows you as Veronica."

I nod. "Yeah…you're right."

I fast-forward through roughly five minutes of silence. "Wow, he kept you guys waiting awhile."

"Uh-huh."

Finally the door opens again.

"I am so sorry for the delay." Ward's voice is low and syrupy, just like I remember it from last night. Hearing his voice again draws me to him and I'm suddenly aware that I'm eager to see him. The desire confuses me. It's hard to put a finger on the sensation—while there is a sexual element to it, it's more than that. It's a yearning to be near him, in the same room as him. I shake my head. *Snap out of it, Sophie.*

Stephen French introduces Sloan and Carey to Anton Ward. "Anything else, master?"

"No, that will be all. Thanks, Stephen."

The door closes.

"Again, please accept my humblest apologies."

Sloan clears her throat purposefully but doesn't say anything.

I hear coffee being poured.

"I'm a night person, you see. So for me, it's now roughly two o'clock in the morning."

"You always been a night person, Mr. Ward?" Sloan asks.

"Since I was fourteen. Most of us are awakened in our adolescence."

"So that'd be about eighteen years ago?" Carey asks.

"As I'm sure you found out from some sort of background search, Detective Carey, I was born on

September 7, 1977. And my birth name was Brett Simons."

"So you don't claim to be a two-hundred-year-old vampire?"

There are a few seconds of silence, and then the sound of a cup being placed on a table. "It is not a simple question that you ask, Ms. Sloan."

"Simple from where I'm sitting." Sloan pauses. "And it's Detective Sloan, thanks."

"I'm sorry." He pauses. "*Detective* Sloan." Another brief pause. "In answer to your question, I am thirty-two years old…in this life. But I have been reincarnated several times and always come into my birthright as a vampire on my fourteenth birthday. But it is not what you think…I'm not delusional, nor must I feed on huge quantities of blood. Vampirism is greatly misunderstood. People base their perception of vampires on books and movies, not on real life."

"Real life?" Sloan keeps her voice open.

"In real life there are some individuals who need the blood of others to survive." He pauses, contemplative. "Or certainly to thrive. A vampire who does not maintain himself in the proper way will find it difficult to even get out of bed, let alone function normally."

"You mean coffin." Now Sloan doesn't hide the amusement in her tone. "Get out of your coffin."

A beat of silence, then: "It is both a condition and a calling, Detective." His voice is slow and forceful.

"I'm sorry, Mr. Ward, but to an outside observer this seems…well, fanciful at best."

"That's ignorance. I will try to explain the feeling in terms you can understand. It's a little like the lack of energy people with glandular fever or severe depression experience." He sighs and I can hear him pick up his cup of coffee and have another sip. "You have a question, Detective Carey."

"That was a little unnerving," Carey says from the front seat.

I turn off the recorder. "How so?"

"I do think this is all baloney, but I really *was* about to ask him a question."

"Your expression probably gave it away, Carey." Sloan throws him a sideways glance. "Let's face it—your poker face isn't the best."

Carey isn't put off by Sloan's dig. "I don't think so."

"Or it was a lucky guess." Sloan snorts. "Next you'll be telling me he sucked your energy."

Carey gives Sloan a fake smile.

I press Play again, ready for Carey's question.

"Yes, Mr. Ward. You said it's a condition. So you're saying that you and your members have a medical condition that means you require blood?"

"Medical and spiritual. Our bodies need the energy of others to thrive. We feed off them, off their life force—either through their blood or spiritually."

"Spiritually?"

"There are two types of vampirism, Detective Carey. One involves feeding from blood and the other type is called psi-vampirism. In the latter, you feed off a person's spiritual energy."

"And what type are you, Mr. Ward?" Sloan's gone back to the serious approach.

"I am both, Detective."

Sloan clears her throat. "And you're the head of After Dark, correct?" A pause, probably while Ward confirms nonverbally, and then Sloan says, "And how many vampires are there in the group?"

"We are a small house. Selective. My clan has nineteen vampires at the moment and ten donors, although we do also associate with others from within L.A.'s vampire community."

"You said *house?*"

"A family, a group, if you like. It can sometimes also be called a clan or coven, but I do not like coven because of its link to witches."

"Vampires don't like witches?"

Ward gives a little exasperated sigh. "Again, I can hear the mockery in your voice. I am not talking about the witches of fiction who cast spells and can fly...or vampires who can only be killed by a stake through the heart. I am referring to the ancient feminine power of Wicca and the condition of vampirism. We don't choose to be a vampire, just like we don't choose the color of our hair—we are born with it."

"And you were born with raven-black hair I suppose?" Sloan's on his back instantly. And again, she's got a point. In the photos and in person last night, Ward's hair was jet-black. There's no way it could be that black...without a little help from a bottle.

He lets out a deep chuckle. "Point taken, Detective Sloan. My analogy is faulty because many people do choose the color of their hair. But I can assure you, *my* hair is natural and so is my vampirism."

"Is the L.A. vampire community a large one?" Sloan brings the conversation back on point.

"Yes. I'd say there are a couple of thousand vampires, maybe more, then the donors and wannabes."

"Wannabes?" Sloan sounds genuinely curious.

"People who are drawn to the image, the mythology, but do not, in fact, need another's life force to survive."

I pause the recording. "That's a lot of suspects."

Sloan nods. "I'll say. Assuming Sherry's death is related to this aspect of her life."

Obviously Sloan's still not sold that our perp is someone from L.A.'s vampire community. I hit Play again.

"And how many houses?" Carey asks.

"It is hard to say. There are many houses in L.A."

"Give us a ballpark, Mr. Ward." Sloan is a little impatient.

"Maybe fifteen houses."

I blow out a breath, but keep the recording going. It is a lot of suspects, but at least it's a little more specific than the information Cheryl was able to give us last night.

"And the donors," Carey asks. "They're the ones who give blood, right?"

"That's correct, Detective."

"Do any of your members live here?" Sloan asks.

We know that at least Riley and Davidson live in their own place, but what about the others? It was a good question, especially from my point of view. Destructive cults tend to be isolated geographically as well as emotionally.

"No. Not full-time. Although some members of my house do stay over from time to time."

"We'd like the names of everyone in After Dark," Sloan says. "Including the donors."

"Do you have a warrant, Detective? I do have the privacy of my family to consider."

"I assumed an upstanding citizen like yourself would want to help the law." Sloan pulls off that perfect balance between friendliness and authority.

"Yes, of course. But you still haven't told me exactly what all this is about. A murder, I believe?"

"Yes. Your butler told you that?"

"Correct. And I believe you were at Walter Riley and Larry Davidson's apartment."

"News travels fast." Sloan's voice is tight.

"Well, the victim is not from my house. So perhaps you think one of us is the killer?"

"What makes you think the victim isn't a member of After Dark?" Sloan asks. It's been less than twenty-four hours since the body was discovered and Ward isn't next of kin…

"I would have felt it, Detective. I am connected to all from my house and would know if one of them had been harmed."

"Like a disturbance in The Force?" Carey asks, his voice even.

The analogy, the joke, is met with silence.

Eventually Ward says, "I know all my members are alive and well. Which brings me back to my question—you think one of us is the killer?" He leaves the question unanswered and continues. "So there must be some evidence of vampirism on the body or at the crime scene."

"That's police business, Mr. Ward," Carey replies.

A pause, then: "Quite. Well, I can assure you it's no one from my house. Our donors must be willing and I do not condone violence or force of any kind."

"I'm afraid we'll need more than your *word*, Mr. Ward," Sloan says.

"No one in my house would dare disobey my rules. I am a kind and generous master. They do not want to be out of my favor."

"That may be the case, Mr. Ward, but this is a murder investigation and we will be talking to all of your members." Sloan's voice is polite but firm. "You can help us, or you can make this less pleasant for all your members we question."

I hear his coffee cup being put down on the table again. "Of course I will help the police. I am hosting a party here tonight. I will arrange for my members to come early, so you can talk to them."

"All members?" Sloan confirms.

"Yes. When I call, they come."

I pause the recording. "I don't think he's using the word *call* in reference to phoning his members. It's more like a master calling for his dog." I stare out the window at the stream of traffic stop-starting in the opposite direction. "And perhaps that's just how he sees his members—as beasts he has trained to obey him." The professional, rational me has enough perspective to see the dynamics, but I can also understand why they come. Most people would jump at any opportunity to be close to Ward. I chew on my bottom lip.

"You're spot-on, Anderson." Carey turns around to see me properly. "It wasn't that he was being derogatory to his members, as such, but it was all just so…matter-of-fact."

I nod and press Play again.

Sloan speaks next. "Thank you, Mr. Ward. That would be most helpful."

"Do you know the identity of the murder victim?"

"Yes. Sherry Taylor. Does the name ring a bell?"

"No."

I hear a slight rustle of paper. Sloan must be showing him Sherry's photo. "This is her."

It's a few seconds before Ward speaks. "She is…was… beautiful. But I've never seen her before."

"She's definitely not one of After Dark's donors?" Sloan asks.

"So she was bitten." It's not a question; it's a statement and his voice is smug, as though he's uncovered a vital piece of information that we were keeping from him.

"Correct, Mr. Ward," Carey says. "But we are keeping that detail from the press. So if you don't mind, please keep it between us."

"Of course. Anything I can do to help. Does eight-thirty this evening suit you? I know it's out-of-office hours, but, like I said, we are creatures of the night."

"That'll be fine," Sloan says. "How do you recruit your members, Mr. Ward?"

"Usually referral…word of mouth. We are a small community, even though L.A. is such a large city."

"And is there a membership fee?"

"A very small administrative fee. But as you can see, Detective Sloan, I do not need money. I am self-made."

Sloan looks back at me and I pause the tape.

"Gosh, I had to bite my tongue on that one. Self-made?" Her left eyebrow arches high above her eye. "Made by Daddy, more like."

I manage a laugh even though I find myself wanting to jump to Ward's defense. Part of me is somehow captured in his spell. I bite my lip again and press Play.

"And what if one of your members wanted to leave?" Carey broaches one of the few questions I'd briefed them to ask. In the classic cult framework, vulnerable individuals are recruited and the leader makes it almost impossible for them to leave. Either physically or financially. And according to Cheryl from Malediction Society, not many have left.

"Any of my clan is welcome to leave. But not many *want* to leave."

"So it has happened?"

"Of course. After Dark has been around for ten years. We've had people come and go."

"We'd like the names of your past members, too, Mr. Ward," Sloan says.

"Certainly. I will bring a list this evening."

"Was Damien Winters the most recent member to leave the group?" Sloan asks.

There's a moment's hesitation, as if the question unsettled him. Perhaps he didn't expect the detectives to know about Winters.

"That's correct, yes."

"And why did Mr. Winters leave?"

"I cannot be certain what caused his ultimate desire, but things had become a little tense between Damien and me, so I'm sure that must have contributed to his decision."

"You had an argument?" I can hear Sloan take a large sip of coffee.

"Not an argument, Detective, no. Damien is a Web developer. Very smart man, and mostly self-taught. However, I didn't agree with some of the clients he was taking on and I told him so."

I manage to bring my analytical self to the fore and pause the tape. "This could be the control element we so often see in a leader of a new religious movement. Ward was trying to tell Winters who he could and couldn't take on as clients and it sounds like Winters wasn't exactly receptive."

Sloan nods. "Yes. I pushed him on it. It's coming up."

I hit Play again.

"You didn't agree? Politically?"

"I guess you could call it that, Detective, but perhaps philosophically would be a more apt description. Damien was getting more and more corporate clients, including a tobacco company and a gambling company."

"Evil?" Sloan braves.

"Social evil, yes, Detective Sloan. I like to protect my members from hardships in this life and I also insist they're free from any addictions—drugs and alcohol of course, but also smoking and gambling. It is hard enough to live the life we do without complicating matters. And I don't approve of organizations that prey on others' weaknesses, feeding their habits."

A sense of admiration washes over me…a socially minded man, keeping an eye out for his friends.

"This is your moral code? And you enforce it on After Dark?" Sloan clarifies.

"*Enforce* is not the word I'd use, but in essence what you're saying is correct." He pauses. "Truth be told, Damien and I were drifting apart. This was simply the last straw, I suppose."

"Any particular reason you were drifting apart?"

He shrugs. "Not really, no. I guess After Dark no longer met Damien's needs."

There's a moment's silence before Sloan moves on to the next topic.

"Can you tell us a little about the After Dark symbol? The pentagram."

"Ah, yes. The pentagram. It does not stand for evil, as many think, Detective Sloan. In fact, the pentagram has a very noble history and was seen as something that protected the wearer from evil. It represents the mastery of the spirit over the four elements—earth, wind, fire and water—and was even worn by Sir Gawain of the Knights of the Round Table."

"And this is what it means in After Dark's context?" Carey asks.

"Correct. After Dark is a home and it is safe. The pentagram represents that safety and protects us, and it symbolizes our connection with the elements."

After a few beats of silence I hear movement, like someone's standing up.

"Thank you for your time," Sloan says.

"You're welcome."

More movement, then Carey says, "Mr. Ward, where do most vampires bite their donors?"

"It depends on the vampire and donor. It's very personal. However, contrary to the fictional vampires, we don't tend to go for the neck. It's simply too dangerous. Vampires who feed on blood do not need very much. They certainly do not need to drain the whole body and kill the donor. Again, that is fiction, not fact." He pauses. "Is there anything else?"

"Yes," Sloan says. "Do you always video your guests?"

"It is part of my security system, Detective Sloan. As I'm sure you can see, I have many valuable objects in this room and I need to protect them." He takes a deep breath. "If there's nothing else, I do need to get *some* sleep."

"One more thing. Do you ever use Temescal Gateway Park or Topanga State Park?"

There's a long pause. "On occasion, yes."

I stop the recording. "He admitted to using the parks."

Carey looks back from the front seat. "Yes, but I don't know if this guy and his group are contenders."

I'm glad I'm not the only one getting the "good guy" vibe off Anton Ward. Even though I still think Sherry's murder has got something to do with vampires.

"I agree," Sloan says. "They're on our radar now, but I want to see how Todd Fischer and Sherry's professor pan out."

Mmm…I'm with her on Ward, but still have to disagree on Fischer. As for Professor Carrington, who knows?

I press Play again and pick up the interview with Sloan asking Ward if he was at the park three months ago when Larry Davidson and Walter Riley were arrested.

There's a long pause. "I confess…we were all there that night. Larry and Walter insisted on keeping After Dark out of the picture. In the end, I decided to respect their loyalty to the group."

"I wonder who *really* insisted that After Dark's name be kept out of the charges," Sloan says over the top of the recording.

I tune back into the interview.

"And when was the last time you and your clan were in Temescal Gateway Park?" Sloan asks.

"About a month ago."

"That was the most recent visit?" Carey presses.

"Yes."

A small pause, before Sloan thanks Ward for his time.

I hear the door open and then Ward says, "Show our guests out. Thank you, Stephen."

"Yes, master."

"The butler was waiting outside?" I ask.

"Uh-huh."

The recording plays a couple of footsteps before they stop and Sloan says, "What size shoe do you wear, Mr. Ward?"

"Twelve."

The loud footsteps resume as Sloan and Carey are shown out.

I hit Stop. "So the shoe sizes are possible matches for Riley, Davidson and Ward."

Carey twists around again. "Yes, but we're only talking partial prints and it's a common size."

I nod. "Anything more specific from the lab?"

"They're in a queue for analysis now. Could be a couple of days."

I move us back to Ward. "Ward's an interesting guy, huh?"

"I'll say." Sloan shakes her head. "There was one moment when he was obviously annoyed with me and I gotta say, I actually found myself wishing I hadn't upset him." Sloan's face crinkles in disgust. "That's not an emotion I'm used to feeling."

"I know what you mean." I'm relieved that Sloan was affected by him, too. "Just from meeting him last night I can see how he attracts his followers *and* keeps them in line." Again, I have to consciously, and with some effort, move myself into analytical mode. "But like most leaders he's probably a master of human behavior. A chameleon... someone who shows you the face you need to see when he's trying to charm you. Then once he's got power over you, you'd do almost anything to keep him happy. To serve him."

"Sounds like some of our politicians." Sloan pulls up at a stoplight.

"All leaders exhibit similar traits. That's what attracts them to positions of power in the first place and helps to keep them there."

"You notice the butler called him master, too?" Carey only partially turns around. "Like Davidson and Riley."

"It's probably simply an old-school approach to the traditional master-servant dynamic rather than the butler being part of Ward's wider house."

Sloan glances at her watch. "We're almost at the coroner's office. I hope we haven't missed the autopsy."

"Me, too." I stare out the window at the dark clouds rolling in from the west. "Bodies always talk."

Nine

Monday, 11:30 p.m.

At the county coroner's office on North Mission, we find Belinda Frost closing up the body in autopsy room four.

She looks up at our entrance. "You missed all the fun."

"Looks like it." Sloan leads the way across the room and stands next to Frost.

Sherry's brown hair looks almost damp, clinging to her body and the gurney in small clumps, and her skin is even paler than I remember from the crime scene. Then again, the bright fluorescent overhead lights certainly accentuate the pastiness. The Y-cut of the autopsy is half closed, with Frost's neat stitches running from Sherry's abdomen to her chest, while the arc from collarbone to collarbone remains open.

"Well?" I stand on the other side of the gurney with Carey next to me. The autopsy may be finished, but at least we can talk to Frost while her findings are fresh in her mind.

"Cause of death is going to be tricky." She sighs. "Like I said yesterday, we've got no medical way of measuring the amount of blood in a body at death, and I haven't found anything else today to indicate cause of death. While the body looked pale at the crime scene, it wasn't exsanguinated." She looks up. "*Exsanguination* is when the body is completely drained of blood. But that wasn't the case here."

"So there's no way to tell if someone drank her blood?" I flick the ring on my little finger, flashing back to the killer biting down on me during my dream on Saturday night.

"No. All I can say is that I can't rule it out. The injury—" she points to Sherry Taylor's neck "—has ruptured the jugular. And the vein has collapsed, indicating some sort of trauma."

"The contusions on her face and arms imply she was traveling through the brush at some speed," Frost says "And with her heart rate elevated, from a slight downward angle an attacker would have been able to see her pulse in the jugular and target it that way. The jugular would provide a strong flow, but not the dramatic spurting you'd get with a severed carotid. And the most someone would get is two to three liters of blood before the jugular collapsed."

"Would that be enough to kill her?"

"Yes. The average person has about five liters in circulation, so you're talking about losing roughly half. She would have gone into hypovolemic shock and her heart rate would increase while her blood pressure dropped. At that point, the brain would be struggling to get the blood it needed. At that stage, her blood pressure would be so low that no more blood would flow from the wound. She'd have only been alive for a few more minutes, ten at the most."

"Unconscious?" I ask.

"Yes. Toward the end."

Sloan stares at Sherry's face. "Thank goodness for small mercies."

Frost grimaces. "The blood flow would have been quite slow. If she did bleed out, she was probably conscious for at least the first ten minutes of the whole ordeal."

We're silent for a bit before Carey says, "So where to from here, Doc?"

"I did find some particles of wood and pollen in the scratches on her arms and face, which I've passed on to the lab for comparison with the plant varieties in Temescal Park and Topanga State Park. But it's safe to assume it'll be a match, given the wounds were fresh."

We all nod.

"Then there's the tox screen. Like I said, there's no way for me to conclusively declare blood loss as the cause of death. But maybe there's something else in the tox screen."

"That won't give us much unless she was poisoned or sedated." In all likelihood the tox screen will just show us that she had alcohol or painkillers in her system, if anything.

"What about the puncture marks?" Sloan points to Sherry's neck. "The bite?"

"Two marks, almost perfectly cylindrical. Whatever punctured the skin was extremely sharp and left no fragments on the skin or surrounding tissue."

"Teeth? Metal?"

She cocks her head to one side. "Could be either. The marks are too far apart for a standard fork." Frost holds up a fork.

Sloan looks at the fork and then at Frost, before arching one eyebrow.

Frost shrugs. "I brought it in from home this morning." She puts the fork against Sherry Taylor's throat, demonstrating the mismatch.

"What about a barbecue fork or serving fork?" I ask.

"I've got my assistant looking into that at the moment. We'll try a few different sizes and see if anything matches."

"And if it's teeth?" Sloan leans in for a closer look at the wound. "It's obviously been made to look like a vampire bite because of the hickey around it."

"Yes. Although if someone was drinking the vic's blood, they would have only needed to suck hard in the last few minutes. Before that the flow would have been strong enough from Sherry's beating heart."

We nod.

She reaches into her pocket. "These are the standard Halloween vampire teeth. The size is roughly correct." She holds the plastic teeth up against Sherry's throat and the alignment is almost perfect. "But obviously these teeth aren't sharp enough to cause that wound, even if they were wielded with great force." She holds the teeth high above the body and brings them down forcefully, stopping short of Sherry's throat. It looks almost comical and I resist the urge to smile.

I focus on the teeth. "Apparently some vampires file their canine teeth to sharpen them, or get caps or dentures."

"Any teeth would have to be extremely sharp and that would cause problems if they were permanent. The person would be cutting their bottom lip on them all the time."

I nod. "So dentures rather than caps."

"Probably."

Carey leans on the gurney. "Looks like we need to talk to some dentists."

"It's most likely an area of specialization," Frost says. "And I'd say it's a word-of-mouth thing with these people. You know, who did your teeth?"

I smile. "Wow, those fangs are great. Where did you get them?"

Frost nods. "Pretty much."

I sigh. "Hate to burst the bubble, but I did a quick Google search and there are lots of providers. Too many to chase down. I actually found quite a few Web sites dedicated to vampires and there are a host of suppliers—from clothes and jewelry to teeth and furniture."

Carey shakes his head. "Who knew the vampire culture was so big?"

A beat of silence.

"I've definitely ruled out snakebite, too. I ran the swabs in the lab and there's no poison present around the wound. Besides, the size doesn't correlate with snake fangs."

"And what about saliva or DNA from the wound?"

"I've sent a cross section from the wound over to DNA, but if there was any saliva present, it must have been a minute amount."

Another beat of silence.

"So if blood loss is our cause of death, was it from *this* wound?" Sloan asks.

"I'd say so, yes. No other wounds and no signs of internal bleeding."

"And only a tiny amount of blood at the scene," I add.

"Yes. That's being run for a DNA comparison with Sherry, but I'm sure we'll find it matches." She waits, giving us time to comment. When we don't she continues, "So the blood was either ingested or pumped into some container."

"Pumped?" Sloan's brow furrows.

"The redness and bruising around the puncture marks indicate a sucking on the skin. But that could have been made by a mouth or by some sort of pump. Much like women use a breast pump when they're breastfeeding."

"Would a breast pump do the job?"

She shakes her head. "Not unless it was fitted with some sort of attachment. A breast pump attaches to a woman's nipple, covering the surrounding area and creating a suction cup. But that suction cup is rounded, in line with a breast's curvature. For the throat—" Frost points to Sherry's wound again "—you'd need a smaller suction area and the cup would have to be flatter. Especially given the wound and the crime scene were so clean."

Silence again.

"Still," she continues, "it wouldn't be hard to adapt a breast pump. Someone could just switch out the suction cup on the end."

"You think that's more likely than someone drinking the blood straight from her throat?" I ask.

"The vic would need to lose two to three liters of blood to cause death. That's a lot of fluid, especially when the body's natural response to ingesting blood is to vomit. It makes sense that at least some of it was saved, unless we're talking about twenty or thirty perps."

I bite my lip. "We could be. Apparently there are thousands of vampires in L.A. and lots of them form houses... hang out together."

Frost shrugs. "So maybe they didn't need a pump." She pauses. "But there is only one bite mark."

"Is it possible one person made the bite and then they all took turns drinking her blood?"

"Possible, yeah. The first few changeovers would be trickier because the blood would have been flowing, but that might account for the drops we found on scene."

"And she wasn't moved postmortem?" I'm wondering if she bled out somewhere else.

Frost shakes her head. "Lividity indicates she died where we found her. The photos of her back match the terrain, with a few rocks making a lividity imprint on her back."

I nod, remembering the case when a perp transported

a body in the trunk of his car, with a spare set of license plates. The red patches on the victim's skin as gravity pulled the blood toward her back showed a lovely partial imprint of a license plate. Body was found, number plate was traced and, voila, killer in custody.

Whether it's two people or thirty, if they all drank Sherry's blood they're equally responsible for her death. The puncture wounds didn't kill her—it was blood loss, presumably. But how can we prove that in a court of law? It sounds like all we've really got, forensically speaking, is the fact that blood loss is at best a probable cause of death, simply because nothing else could be found. Will Sherry's pale skin and pale internal organs be enough to convince a jury?

"So if the crime scene has been *staged* to look like a vampire attack, our perp would have used a pump," Sloan says.

"Yup. You'll have the official report by midday tomorrow, and the tox screen should come through at some stage tomorrow afternoon."

"Okay. Thanks, Doc." Sloan heads for the door while Belinda Frost goes back to her suturing.

Sloan sets a fast pace along the corridors, surprisingly fast given her size and age. Guess she's in a hurry to get out. The full gurneys that line the corridor don't exactly make you want to stick around, but it's been like this ever since I've been working out of L.A. The first time I visited the coroner's office I was shocked—most places have enough room to keep the dead who are waiting for an autopsy in the slide-out cabinets, but the L.A. Coroner's Office is in desperate need of an extension or total relocation. Who knows what they'd do if the air-conditioning malfunctioned.

"You remember a time when it wasn't like this?" I ask Sloan.

She looks at me questioningly.

"The bodies."

"Oh. Sure. But we're talking maybe twenty years ago. L.A.'s dead outgrew this place over a decade ago."

"How long have you been working Homicide here?"

She slows down a little. "I was with the Los Angeles Sheriff's Department from 1978 to 1998. Worked Homicide for fifteen of that twenty, until my retirement in 1998. I took a couple of years off before signing up at the LAPD."

"Sucker for punishment." Carey smiles.

"I was just happy the LAPD didn't mind hiring an old gal like me."

"Law enforcement can always use experienced officers," I say.

"Ain't that the truth. Especially when most of us are only in it for twenty years."

"I'm surprised you didn't contract back for the LASD." The Sheriff's Department often hires back its homicide detectives as contractors, and they have a strong homicide department because of this strategy. LAPD's jurisdiction covers the City of Los Angeles, which equates to over three million residents and 465 square miles. And they have roughly 9,200 officers to police that area. The Sheriff's Department polices most of the rest of L.A. county—with a few exceptions—covering two and a half million people across 3.101 square miles. While their jurisdiction is larger, they have fewer sworn officers at roughly 8,400.

"I wanted a change of scenery. Wanted to dig my teeth into the city. But I would have taken the offer up if LAPD hadn't panned out."

We exit the cream building and walk the one hundred feet to Sloan's car.

"Carrington next?" Carey asks.

Sloan looks up at the sky, like she's using the sun's position to tell the time. "Too early."

"I wouldn't mind heading back to the office for a bit. I want to set myself up online, as Veronica, and I also want to see what the American Psychological Association and American Psychiatry Society say about Renfield's syndrome." I look at Sloan. "Plus I will talk to my boss about the undercover angle. Play it by the book." I use Sloan's terminology.

She gives me a cursory nod. "Carey and I need to work on Sherry's missing hours, 9:00 p.m. to midnight, assuming Todd's telling us the truth. Any word from Bar Sinister on the video footage?"

I dig out my BlackBerry. "Nope. I'll chase them again this afternoon. And I'm still waiting to hear back from the manager at Monte Cristo for video footage of Ruin and Malediction Society."

"It sure would be nice to know if Sherry was at Bar Sinister on Saturday night." She leans on the car. "Credit card and phone records should be in soon, too."

"It's going to be a busy day." I open the car door, eager to get on the road.

Sloan's still leaning on the car in thought. "Why don't you pass over the video tasks to Carey? That'll give you more time to focus on the online leads and the vamps."

I could do with more time. "Sure. If that's okay?" I look to Carey who gives me a shrug and then a nod.

We all get in the car and once we're on the move I say, "I've got the FBI computer guys working on Sherry's computer, and they can probably help out with the video footage when it comes in."

"Might be an idea. Sounds like our tech guys are swamped. Carey, can you please—"

My mobile phone interrupts Sloan but I let it ring while she finishes her sentence.

"—chase down the footage and send it over to the FBI once you get it."

Carey gives a nod as I answer the call.

"Special Agent Anderson."

"Hi. It's Brad Razor from the Monte Cristo. You left a message."

Speak of the devil. "Thanks for returning the call. We came in last night and spoke to your bar manager about After Dark and a few of your other customers."

"Yup, Cheryl told me."

"We're interested in getting more information about some of your clients. Maybe from the bar tabs, credit card receipts or your mailing list."

"Um…I don't know about that. Don't you need a warrant or something? I don't think my customers would like it if I gave out their details."

"We understand, Mr. Razor. But a young woman's been murdered. Anything you can do to help us would be greatly appreciated."

He hesitates. "I don't know."

"Cheryl mentioned three guys and a woman who come in. One of the guys dresses like *Clockwork Orange*."

"I know them."

"Maybe if you could just give us their names…it'd be most helpful."

"The ones you're talking about, they're all friends on our Malediction Society MySpace page. But I don't know their real names, only their user IDs. They don't have a tab and if they've ever used credit cards I wouldn't be able to match their real names to the names I know them by anyway."

I guess that's fair enough. "Okay. I'll check out the MySpace page and track them down from there." I pause. "We noticed you had a few video cameras in the club. Do you keep the footage?"

"Uh-huh, but only for a month or two."

"We'd like all the footage from the past two months." I'm hoping Brad Razor isn't going to force us down the warrant route for the video, too.

He's silent for a bit.

"This is a murder investigation, Mr. Razor. And it's not customers' names and addresses we're asking for. Besides, this is precisely why video cameras exist, no?"

"Okay, okay."

"Thanks. We'll send someone over to pick up the discs. Do you ever get much trouble in the club?"

"Not really, no."

"So there's no one in particular you think we should focus on?"

"Most of my clientele are very well behaved, Agent."

"Okay. I'll check out your MySpace friends. Thanks, Mr. Razor."

"No names?" Sloan asks once I've hung up.

"No. But apparently they're friends on Malediction Society's MySpace page. I doubt we'd get probable cause for a search warrant at this stage."

"Damn system makes it too hard."

Probable cause *can* make things hard for law enforcement, but I'm not going to get into a debate with Sloan or anyone else on personal privacy versus law-enforcement's discretionary powers. It's a never-ending argument.

I shrug. "It's okay. At least he's giving us the video footage." I stare out the window. "We should check out Damien Winters today, too. See what his story is."

"Let's not forget Todd Fischer and Professor Carrington." Sloan pulls onto North Mission.

"I know we can't ignore some of the standard murder scenarios, but we've got a circle of candles, potential fang marks on the body and blood loss as the most likely cause of death, plus we've got Sherry's recent involvement in the Goth scene." Why did Sloan call me in if she wasn't going to take this angle seriously? I cross my arms, knowing all too well the answer—she was covering her bases. No matter what happens now, she can say she got the Feds involved and a profiler on the case.

"Heeler and his circle of candles…the guy's a drunk. Who knows what he saw? And I'm still not convinced someone didn't stage the other elements."

I resist the urge to blow out a sigh of frustration but I think my silence is enough of a response.

Sloan gives me a tight smile in the rearview mirror. "Let's see what the professor and Desiree have got to say this afternoon, huh?"

At the Cyber Crime Division I sit with Mercedes.

"You don't look that tired," I say.

"I'm not too bad. I didn't get up for the gym this morning, though."

"Me neither."

"So, you want to use one of those pics I took last night?"

"Yeah."

"I haven't downloaded them yet, but I remembered to bring in the camera." Mercedes pulls out her small digital camera from her handbag. Once the photos are downloaded, we go through them.

"I like this one." She gives me a little smile.

"I don't think so." She's picked one that shows the most flesh. "Besides, head and shoulders is best, right?"

"Yeah. Or I could do you up a little graphical icon. Lots of people do it online anyway, so it won't look out of place."

"Let's go with the icon and then we can upload one of these pics into the photos area."

"Good call." Even as she speaks, she's typing and multiple screens are flashing up in front of her face. Within a couple of minutes she's got three icons on screen. "One of these should do the job. What do you think?"

The first graphic is a cartoon-style version of a bat— clichéd but descriptive. The second one is a woman's face, with fangs. And the third one is a bite mark, blood oozing on a white background.

"Let's go with the face," I say. "It's kinda cute."

She smiles. "If you like that sort of thing."

"Which our target audience does."

Within less than a minute she's set up a Yahoo account under the username LadyVeronica, and she's routed the confirmation e-mail to a dummy Bureau account we use for our online activities. Next, it's onto Facebook, where she registers and starts setting up the page.

"Date of birth?"

"The youngest I can get away with…twenty-eight?"

"Easy."

"Thanks." Like many women over thirty, I don't mind shaving a few years off my real age. "Any date is fine."

"Okay." Mercedes enters May 22 and selects 1982 as the year. Even though the year is optional, why not give Anton Ward and other viewers the age of our character? And judging by After Dark's female members, he likes them in their twenties.

For location we put L.A., obviously, and list most of the vampire novels, films and TV shows under the respective sections.

"We don't need to fill out too much information," says Mercedes. "Just enough to give Veronica a presence."

"Maybe we should set one up for you, too? Realistically, both Veronica and Crystal would be on Facebook and they'd be friends."

"Yeah, you're right. I'll set up some extra profiles that we can friend, too. It would look pretty lame if Veronica and Crystal only had one friend each."

"Good point."

It takes Mercedes less than ten minutes to create her own Facebook profile as Crystal and set up twenty additional dummy profiles, linking them all up.

"So, friend requests." Mercedes looks to me for some names.

"Detectives Sloan and Carey will be getting a full list of the members of After Dark tonight, but I think we should start with Anton Ward and the two girls we met last night."

"Uh-huh."

"Besides, it should be a natural growth. It would be suspicious if we suddenly sent friend requests to all the After Dark members."

"Sure." She keeps typing.

"And we can send requests to the clubs, too, or sign up for their pages."

She nods and does a search for Anton Ward in my fake Facebook page. "There he is." She clicks on *Add Friend*. "Do you want to send a message?"

"Yeah. Say, 'It was great meeting you last night. Can't wait to see you tonight.'"

Mercedes types it in. "So you're definitely going?"

"I've just cleared it with Brady. The paperwork is doing the rounds."

"Official undercover operation?"

"Not exactly. We're still not sure where we're going to take it. But I've got formal permission to go tonight and to set up an online profile." I roll my eyes. "At least it'll get Detective Sloan off my back."

"She's been giving you a hard time?" Mercedes types in the verification words and hits *Okay*.

"Kinda. She thinks I'm taking the vampire angle too seriously for this stage of the investigation."

"And are you?"

I give her a little punch on the arm. "No." I sigh. "Well, I don't think so." I can't tell Mercedes or Sloan about my dream, so maybe from an outsider's point of view it does look like I'm putting all my eggs in one basket.

Mercedes gives me a little smile. "You're just enjoying the research."

I am enjoying the research, and that worries me. But instead of admitting that, I make a joke out of it. "All in the line of duty."

She lets out a little giggle. "The things we have to do." She turns her attention back to the screen. "I'll send a request to Anton from me, too."

"Anton, is it? Could it be that you're enjoying the research?"

She laughs. "Maybe." Once she's logged in as Crystal, she sends Ward a friend request. "Okay. Next are Teresa and Paula. Except we don't know their surnames."

"Oh, yeah." I lean back in the chair. "So maybe we need to wait until we can view Ward's full profile. Then we can contact them."

Mercedes shakes her head. "We can lift their names off MySpace. You don't have to be official friends to view someone's profile on MySpace...unless it's locked."

"Cool."

Mercedes opens a new window and sets up two My-Space pages for us under our aliases. From there she sends friend requests to Anton Ward, Malediction Society, Bar Sinister and Ruin.

She brings up Ward's MySpace profile and starts sorting through the friends, looking for Paula and Teresa. "Here's Teresa. Says her last name is Somers." Mercedes sends MySpace requests for us both and within a few seconds she's back in Facebook doing a search for Teresa Somers. It doesn't take her long to find the right girl. "Want to say anything in this friend request?"

"Just 'Nice to meet you last night.'"

Mercedes nods and types in the message before clicking *Okay*. She goes through the same procedure on her Facebook page before moving back to MySpace and looking for Paula. She finds her quickly—Paula Torres—and soon Veronica and Crystal have sent Paula friend requests, too.

"Done." Mercedes smiles. "The Bureau's e-mail account is automated and I've set it up so all alerts for Veronica will be rerouted to your personal Bureau account and the ones for Crystal to me. That way we can keep on top of the responses, wall posts, etc. It'll come straight into your BlackBerry."

"Sounds great." I pause. "That's it?"

"Uh-huh."

"If only all my leads were that easy to check off."

Mercedes smiles. "Now you know why I like computers so much."

"Because it's not reality?"

"It's just a different reality, that's all."

I stand up and arch my back, stretching. "Hey, any luck with Sherry Taylor's computer?"

Mercedes looks over the corrals. "Steve?"

A few rows over Steve pops up. "Yo."

"How you going with Sherry Taylor? You got that one, right?"

"Uh-huh. I'm working on it now."

"And?" Mercedes walks us over to his desk.

"Usual stuff. I've managed to get into her e-mail accounts, one with AOL and one with Yahoo. Plus MySpace, Facebook and Twitter of course."

"Anything?" I ask.

"Steve Cooper, meet Agent Anderson, profiler."

"Sure. You logged the request."

"That's right."

"I'll have my report to you by tomorrow, but I can show you what I've got so far if you like."

"Sounds great."

"Okay." He takes a breath. "E-mails. Any names in particular you want to look at right now?"

"How about e-mails from the past two weeks to or

from Desiree Jones." I still want to know why Desiree omitted Sherry's crush on the professor from our conversation, not to mention their interest in the Goth culture. It might be handy to go to this afternoon's interview armed with correspondence between the two girls.

Cooper is fast, maybe even faster than Mercedes, and soon he looks up at me. "Printing now. Anyone else? Boyfriend?"

"Yeah, see if there's anything from Todd Fischer." That'll keep Sloan happy at least. "And any luck with the mystery date on Saturday night?" In the request, I'd mentioned that Sherry was supposed to be meeting a guy on Saturday night. Maybe something in her laptop will tell us who.

"Nothing on that yet, I'm afraid. But I'll keep looking." He pauses. "I've got one e-mail from Todd Fischer and Sherry's reply. Printing now. Anything else?"

"Um…have you got her MySpace, Facebook and Twitter login details? I wouldn't mind checking out those accounts, too."

"I can copy the contents onto our server for you, but it won't be interactive. It's better if we don't have too many people accessing her actual account, so we can maintain its integrity."

"Sure." Something from one of the social networking sites may be required in court, and the chain of evidence requirements are a little different for computer and online evidence. I can understand that Cooper doesn't want some computer hack like me fooling around with Sherry's details in real time.

He gets my Bureau username. "Okay, I'll copy those across and give you a call to take you through the access procedure from your computer."

"Great, thanks."

Back at my desk I open up the MySpace page for Malediction Society and spend thirty minutes tracking down the four vampires that Cheryl described, but none of them use their real names. The voluptuous woman is called VampBaby, the big guy with the tat is SirJonas, the *Clockwork Orange* guy is called Kaos and the final of the four is KillerFangs. I e-mail links to each person's profile page through to Mercedes and ask her if she can find out their real names. But in the meantime, I log in as Veronica and send friend requests to the four of them. It's a start at least.

I spend the next hour poring over e-mails between Desiree and Sherry, but they're mostly inane—same with her Facebook, Twitter and MySpace accounts. She doesn't seem to have any online friends through these accounts linked to the Goth world.

Once I'm Facebooked out, I move on to Renfield's syndrome. I find no mention of it in the databases of the American Psychological Association or the American Psychiatric Society or their journals—it's certainly not a clinically recognized disorder.

At 2:00 p.m. an e-mail comes in from Mercedes. She's managed to get names on the rogue four—James Logan, Patricia Peters, Jake Oliva and Jon Eriksson. Mercedes has also performed a DMV search and criminal record search for each of them. I print out the material. Are these our killers?

Ten

UCLA is right around the corner, so when Sloan rings to say they'll be leaving soon I mention I'll walk, which leaves Sloan in shock. Driving everywhere is one part of the American culture I can't imagine ever succumbing to—even a twenty-minute walk is considered too far by many. The people of L.A. may like their exercise, but getting from point A to B is all about the car.

I make my way to Westwood Village, enjoying the sunshine. As I glance up at the sun and soak in its rays, I can't help but think about Anton Ward and his followers. Light sensitivity is one of the many claims of most modern-day vampires, but I don't know how anyone could dislike or avoid the sun—I could certainly never embrace being a creature of the night, that's for sure. But maybe that's the Australian in me. I like my wide-open spaces and blue skies with the sun beating down on me.

I make a quick stop for a soy caramel macchiato at Starbucks, and by the time I'm at the main UCLA entrance less than ten minutes later my cup is empty. On the campus map I look up the location of Jeffrey Carrington's class, the Black Box Theater in Macgowan Hall.

Once I find it, I think maybe I should have driven—the theater is in the northwest corner of the campus and I'm standing on the southern border. Setting a fast pace, I make my way to the theater. Sloan is waiting for me at the entrance.

"Sorry I'm late." My skin is slick with droplets of sweat.

"Just got here myself."

"Where's Carey?"

"I kept him on the video footage. It looks we'll have all the footage to your FBI contact by the end of the day or tomorrow morning at the latest."

"That's great."

We make our way through the main entrance, which takes us in at the back of the small auditorium. About forty students sit in the theater seats, and standing in front of the stage is an older man. On stage, three students act out a scene, and it's soon obvious that one student is a psychiatrist and the other two are patients. One boy's doing a great job of exhibiting classic schizophrenia symptoms and the other one seems to be suffering severe depression. We watch for another minute or so before I spot Desiree in the front row.

"What's Desiree doing here?" I whisper. Yesterday Desiree was shattered by her best friend's murder but today she's come to class? Most people would need a little more time to mourn for the dead.

Sloan raises an eyebrow. "Let's take her first."

We make our way down the center aisle to the teacher.

"Mr. Carrington?" I say.

He turns around, annoyed, and gives us a fervent "Shhh." The students hesitate for only a moment before continuing with their piece, but the boy playing the schizophrenic only gets a few words out before Sloan interrupts again.

"LAPD, Mr. Carrington."

He turns around again, and this time Sloan's holding her badge up in front of his face.

His body slumps, like he's lost one of his best friends. "Sherry."

"Yes. We're investigating her murder." Sloan introduces us both.

Now the rest of the class has their attention firmly focused on us, not the stage.

Desiree sits front and center, with another two girls on either side of her. I give her a nod and she responds with a hesitant, self-conscious smile like she doesn't want everyone to know we've already spoken.

I decide to push the matter to observe her response. "Hi, Desiree. How are you?"

She looks down, something uncharacteristic for a girl of her obvious confidence. "Okay, thanks."

Maybe it's grief.

Now all eyes are on her and she doesn't seem comfortable with that. Maybe she's not as outgoing and confident as Mrs. Taylor thinks, or as she first appeared to me.

"The class is devastated by Sherry's death." Carrington's hands clasp together and he brings them up under his chin.

"I can see that." Sloan looks around at the class.

Carrington either doesn't pick up on her sarcasm or ignores it. Instead his brow wrinkles. "*I'm* devastated. Sherry…" He shakes his head and looks off into the distance. "I'm close to all my students."

A quick glance around the room shows a few of the females looking up at Carrington with adoring eyes, including Desiree. I don't see the attraction myself, but then I'm not a college girl. And what exactly does "close" mean?

"I'm sorry for your loss," I say politely.

He nods and the students look appropriately somber. But they are all actors…or studying to be.

I give him a small smile. "We'd like a few words with Desiree, and then you, Mr. Carrington."

"Of course. Anything I can do to help you find Sherry's killer." More brow wrinkling.

Maybe I'm being unjustifiably harsh.

I turn my attention back to Desiree and give her a nod. She grabs a leather satchel from the floor and presses past her friends.

"We were so looking forward to Sherry's performance today, too." Carrington sighs. "She's always exceptional… artistry to watch." A tear glistens in the corner of his eye.

Nope, I wasn't being harsh—the man's a piece of work. This whole thing is a performance for us, and his students. Can't wait to question him…maybe Sloan's on the money looking into Sherry's romantic involvements first and foremost. But Carrington will keep for a few minutes.

We lead Desiree up the stairs, away from prying ears. "Where can we go that's private?" I ask.

She shrugs. "There may be a classroom free. Or at this time the Murphy Sculpture Garden won't be too busy. At least for another fifteen minutes."

"Great. Lead the way."

We follow Desiree into the sculpture garden. While there are several groups of students who obviously don't have classes, the place is relatively deserted.

I make for a seat in dappled sunlight. "I'm surprised you're here today, Desiree."

She sits down and bites her fingernails. "I wasn't going to come." She catches herself out and pulls her hand down. "But I know what this class and Jeffrey meant to Sherry. She wouldn't want me to miss it."

Who knows what the dead would want. I think I'd

want my best friend to mourn me for a little longer than a day.

"And Sherry would have wanted me to tell Jeffrey personally, and the class."

I wonder if it's common to use professors' first names at UCLA.

"So you informed them?" Sloan takes a seat next to me.

"I told Jeffrey before the class. He took it even harder than I expected."

"He and Sherry were close?"

"She was his favorite. She's the best in the class by far."

"I see." Sloan pauses. "But their relationship was only student-teacher?"

She hesitates.

"Sherry's dead, Desiree." Sloan speaks softly. "Someone murdered her and your loyalty to her now needs to be directed at catching her killer, not keeping her secrets."

Desiree nods. "I know." A deep breath, then: "Jeffrey's the reason Sherry broke up with Todd. Sherry was in love with him."

So far she's only confirming Todd's story.

"Was the feeling mutual?" I ask.

"Love?" She shakes her head. "I don't think so."

"Did they have a sexual relationship?" Sloan gets straight to the point.

Another pause. "Yes. It started about a month ago." She bites her nails again. "I've got him into so much trouble, haven't I?"

"Sherry's not a minor, so it's not a legal problem." Sloan unbuttons her jacket and leans back, settling in. "But I assume the college has policies about this."

Desiree nods. "And then there's his wife, too."

He's married. Interesting that he doesn't wear his wedding ring...at least not in classes.

"Was there anything else you were hiding from us yesterday?" I ask. Desiree may think the relationship is a revelation to us, but if Davidson and Riley are right, Desiree was not only privy to Sherry's involvement in the Goth world but also a part of it. What if they were donors?

She shakes her head, but it's not a convincing denial.

"So you and Sherry have never been to Bar Sinister?" Sloan's tone is harsh.

"Oh my gosh, how did you know? Was it one of those freaks? Is that who killed her?"

"It's too early to speculate, Desiree." Sloan cocks her head to one side. "But you're not making our job any easier. Why didn't you tell us about this yesterday?"

"I didn't think it was relevant."

Sloan's eyes narrow. "Why on earth not? Any recent changes to someone's lifestyle are extremely important."

Desiree shrugs and bites her fingernails.

In her defense, we didn't mention the bite marks, and thinking back we didn't explicitly ask her about the Goth scene. Maybe it is an innocent oversight on her part.

I rest my hand on Desiree's shoulder. "Tell us about Bar Sinister. Help us bring Sherry's killer to justice."

Desiree puts her head in her hands for a few moments before sitting upright again. "Yes, we were at that bar once, and also Malediction Society. But we're not like them. We're not Goths." Desiree's voice is full of disgust and prejudice. She's ashamed people will find out about her secret.

"But you were dressed as Goths?"

"Yes. The piece we were supposed to perform today… it's about two female Goths who get involved with this creepy guy who thinks he's a vampire."

"So you and Sherry were at the club…"

"Researching. Trying to get a feel for the characters. It's part of method acting."

I've heard about method acting—apparently it's responsible for Dustin Hoffman not showering or sleeping for two days before the climactic scene in *Marathon Man*. Could Sherry's research have cost her her life somehow?

"And what about the other student in the piece?" Sloan asks.

"Gordon. He didn't bother showing up. Decided he didn't need to check out the clubs, but Jeffrey's all about character research. We knew our performances would be way better for inside knowledge. And that Jeffrey would be impressed."

"So the research was to please him?" Sloan's voice is pleasant and conversational again.

She shrugs. "I guess…in a way. The research was to ensure we gave the best performance possible, and that is what pleases Jeffrey. You heard him in there describing Sherry." She jerks her head back toward the classroom. "Artistry. That's the highest compliment coming from Jeffrey."

"I see." Sloan moves forward, leaning her forearms on her thighs. "Did anybody else know about Sherry's affair with Professor Carrington?"

Desiree winces. "It sounds so…sordid when you put it like that."

"Sherry was having an affair with her college professor, Desiree," I say. "They're the facts."

"You don't approve."

I think about it…do I disapprove? Is Desiree overreacting or is she picking up on a judgmental streak in me? Sherry and Carrington are adults. The only part to judge is Carrington's adultery, and that's between him and his wife.

"I don't disapprove, Desiree. My job is to find out

everything I can about a victim and everyone around them. Like I said, I'm just stating the facts. Sherry and Carrington were having a secret relationship and Carrington's married—that fits my definition of an affair." I pause. "Did Sherry see it differently?"

Desiree snorts. "Of course. She believed they were soul mates. That it was only a matter of time before Jeffrey realized Sherry was his true love and left his wife."

Ah, the innocence of youth. I could be wrong, could be showing my jaded, cynical side, but my bet is Sherry isn't Carrington's first.

"What about you, Desiree?" Sloan leans in closer. "Anything between you and Jeffrey Carrington?"

Desiree blushes again. "I wish."

I nod, acknowledging her desire even though I can't see the attraction. I move on to the After Dark group. "Desiree, have you ever heard of Anton Ward, Walter Riley or Larry Davidson?"

She shakes her head.

"What about a group of vampires called After Dark?"

"No."

I pull out pictures of the three men from the case file. Those of Riley and Davidson are mug shots from their arrest, and the photo of Ward is from the newspaper article. "Do you recognize any of these men?"

She looks at the photos and then shakes her head. "No."

"Are you sure? These two men saw you and Sherry at Bar Sinister. They ID'd Sherry. Are you sure you don't recognize them?"

She studies them more closely. "I don't think so. But we talked to lots of people. It gave me the creeps and I just wanted to get the hell out of there, but Sherry wanted to soak up the atmosphere and get an inside take." Desiree shakes her head again. "Looks like she took it too far, huh?"

I'm struck by the coldness of Desiree's last comment. It's almost as if she's insinuating that Sherry deserved what she got. Desiree's hit a nerve with me, but I make sure I don't show it. The she-deserved-it attitude toward victims of sexual assault and sometimes murder works me into a frenzy.

"Did Sherry ever go to the club without you? Or meet up with Goths?"

"I don't think so. But she sure was intrigued by it. Like she thought it was sexy."

"Do you think it's sexy?"

She shrugs. "Some of the vampire books and movies are pretty cool, but I don't want anyone to bite me."

"And Sherry did?"

She hesitates. "She did say she'd like to know what it felt like. That maybe it would be nice."

"How did you respond?"

"I told her she was losing her mind."

I nod. "When was that? When did she express this interest?"

She scrunches up her face. "About a week ago I guess."

"And your last trip to one of the clubs?"

"Malediction Society, eight days ago." She pauses, trying to figure out times. "Yeah, that's right. Sherry wanted to go to Ruin on Friday night, but I said no. When she was trying to convince me to go, Sherry said she wondered what it would be like to be bitten. That maybe it'd be sexy...turn her on."

"Were those her exact words?" Sloan breaks her silence.

"Man...*exact words?*" She takes a few moments. "Yeah, she said it sounded pretty sexy and that it might be a turn-on. I think she mentioned 'exciting,' too. It was like a one-minute conversation."

"We understand. Thanks, Desiree." A glance at my watch tells me class is about to end, and I want to be waiting for Carrington, rather than giving him any more time to mentally rehearse his responses.

I stand up. "Do you think Sherry went to Bar Sinister on Saturday night? That maybe she was going there with her mystery date?"

"It's possible, I guess. She was pretty keen." Desiree stands up.

"Do you think her date was a Goth?"

"It would explain why she didn't tell me who she was hooking up with…she knew I wasn't crazy about the whole scene." She rubs her hand along her thigh. "So, yeah, it's quite possible. Maybe she was even planning on being his donor that night."

Sherry ended up being someone's donor all right, but I keep my mouth shut and start us walking back to the Black Box Theater.

"Anything else you think may be relevant?" Sloan asks. "I'm sure I don't need to remind you that we will find out if there's anything else you're hiding."

"You know everything now." She bites her fingernails. "I've got Jeffrey into so much trouble."

"You've done the right thing, Desiree. Your information may be crucial to finding Sherry's killer." I put my hand on her shoulder. "We want to find whoever did this to her…justice for Sherry."

She nods. "I want you to nail the bastard."

Now that's more the reaction I'd expect from a victim's best friend.

Students spill from Macgowan Hall into the gardens and I quicken my step. Back in the theater, I'm happy to discover that Carrington's running overtime. He sits on the stage, his students all seated in the first few rows of the small theater—a captive audience. He looks up as we enter and gives us a nod. If he's squirming in his boots he's not showing it. It doesn't look like he's worried that Desiree's spilled the beans about his affair with Sherry. Or maybe he assumes Sherry didn't tell anyone...even her best friend.

He wraps up the class by reminding everybody that next week is the two-minute monologue. While some of the students file out immediately, other pupils anxiously await a few minutes of his time. Sloan and I hold our ground at the door, until Desiree's front-row friends flow into the corridor, Desiree in tow. There are still four students, all female, with Carrington, but we wander down the steps and sit a few rows back, waiting for him but eavesdropping at the same time. While all the students have questions about the monologues, I get the feeling that some of them are just using that as an excuse to talk to Carrington.

It's ten minutes before Carrington is finally done. "Sorry, ladies."

I smile. "That's fine. I can see you're in demand."

He nods. "I'm committed to my students, and giving them time is how they improve."

"Of course." But I think it's a mutually beneficial exchange, with Carrington getting more than his fair share in ego boosts. Not to mention lining up women for his extramarital activities.

"So, you'd like to talk to me? About Sherry?"

"Yes."

"This room's free or my office is just around the corner if you'd like to talk there."

I'm interested in Carrington's office—it will give me a better insight into the man. "Your office would be great."

"Right." He gathers up a few files and leads the way. As we walk along the corridors, Carrington receives a healthy amount of female attention. Could he be having affairs with all of them? I doubt it, but I would be surprised if Sherry had been his only extracurricular partner.

Carrington's office is a strange mixture of modern-chic and old-world; like he's tried to marry the two stereotypes of "professor" and "L.A. actor." The furniture, which would presumably be standard college issue, is simply a large wooden desk with an office chair behind it and two comfortable but plain chairs in front of it. In the corner are a filing cabinet and a coat stand. But Carrington's personal touch is evident everywhere else in the room. Firstly, the walls are a shrine—to him. There are both color and black-and-white photos of Carrington on stage, with reviews and newspaper clippings framed and on display. There are also a few photos of Carrington on set; in one he's standing with Mel Gibson, in another Harrison Ford. The photos aren't recent—both Ford and Gibson look significantly younger. Harrison Ford's wearing the trademark *Indiana Jones* hat, so we're probably talking the first or second movie in the series.

Carrington follows my gaze. "That's on the set of *Raiders of the Lost Ark*. With Harrison Ford."

I guess it would be some pickup line: I was in *Raiders of the Lost Ark*. But Carrington's holding on to the past, on to past achievements, and if anything it's amusing... or maybe sad. Not only has he placed the photo directly behind him, but he feels the need to name-drop, too.

"And that's Mel and me from the first *Lethal Weapon*."

Given I don't recognize Jeffrey Carrington, his roles were probably small, but he must have been more than an extra to get a photo with the star.

I give him a little nod. "So, Sherry." I'm silent for a bit, leaving space for Carrington to come in.

He obliges. "Terrible tragedy. That girl had talent."

Sloan crosses her legs and leans into one side of the chair. "So we've heard."

He shakes his head. "If it wasn't for that father of hers, she would have already had a blossoming film or TV career."

"Her father was strict?" Sloan asks.

"When it came to Sherry's acting, yes. With his contacts and her talent she could have been famous and independently wealthy by sixteen. Younger even."

"That's what she wanted? Fame and fortune?"

He puts his forefinger on his bottom lip. "Actually, no. She wanted to be an actor, a serious actor. I don't think she cared about the fame, and she certainly didn't need to worry about money."

"I see." I lean back in my chair and also cross my legs. "Can you tell us more about your relationship with Sherry?"

He moves uncomfortably in his seat, but I get the feeling it's a deliberate movement rather than an unconscious gesture. He purses his lips and then nods slowly. "I guess it'll come out eventually." He takes a deep breath. "Sherry and I had a sexual relationship."

"Really?" I force a small sense of surprise into my voice. "Was it serious?"

"No, definitely not. We'd seen each other a few times, but it was purely sexual."

"When was the first time you slept together?" Sloan asks.

"I don't know. Couple weeks ago maybe." He pauses. "Perhaps three."

Desiree says four weeks, and Carrington says two or three. Not that much of a discrepancy.

"One thing."

"Let me guess, you're worried we'll tell your wife." Sloan doesn't hide a smile.

"My wife? Not at all. We have an open relationship. She knows I see other women."

Now Carrington's managed to shock me.

"It's the dean I'm worried about." He leans over his desk and lowers his voice. "Strictly speaking we're not supposed to have such contact with our students."

Guess he should have thought about that sooner.

"We'll have to see how the investigation pans out." The smile's gone from Sloan's face.

He nods, but only seems slightly worried.

"Do you know how Sherry felt about your relationship?" I ask.

"What do you mean?"

"Did she understand it was only sex?" Sloan dives in feet-first, as usual.

"Of course. I made that very clear from the start."

"Really?" Sloan arches her left eyebrow. "She told Desiree that you were soul mates. That it was only a matter of time before you left your wife for her."

He laughs, but then tempers his reaction. "Sherry was smarter than that. She knew exactly what we had." For the first time he's not so confident.

"You're sure of that?" He's not sure at all.

"I guess…I guess maybe she was falling for me. After our last…meeting I wondered if it was time to break it off. She was giving me the look." He says it with distaste.

"What look?"

He clears his throat. "You're right. She was blurring the line on our relationship. But I don't see what that's got to do with her murder."

"We need to find out as much as we can about Sherry," I say.

Sloan takes out her pen, notebook and reading glasses. "Including her sexual partners."

He sighs. "Go on then."